"I'm not bitter."

The tone of Nathan's voice forced Polly to believe him.

"The boatyard was to be my inheritance and I got it back. But in case you're wondering, no, I *didn't*."

She gazed at him blankly. "No, you didn't what?"

"Make my fortune by cheating others. I'm a hard man, Polly. Some call me ruthless. But when I don't sleep at night, it's not my conscience that keeps me awake."

Dana James lives with her husband and three children in a converted barn on the edge of a Cornish village. She has written thrillers, historical romances and doctor-nurse romances but is now concentrating her efforts on writing contemporary romance fiction. In addition to extensive researching, which she adores, the author tries to write for at least four hours every day.

Books by Dana James

HARLEQUIN ROMANCE
2841—THE MARATI LEGACY
2872—THE EAGLE AND THE SON
2926—TARIK'S MOUNTAIN
2973—SNOWFIRE
2992—POOL OF DREAMING
3068—LOVE'S RANSOM

Don't miss any of our special offers. Write to us at the following address for information on our newest releases.

Harlequin Reader Service
P.O. Box 1397, Buffalo, NY 14240
Canadian address: P.O. Box 603,
Fort Erie, Ont. L2A 5X3

BAY OF RAINBOWS
Dana James

Harlequin Books

TORONTO • NEW YORK • LONDON
AMSTERDAM • PARIS • SYDNEY • HAMBURG
STOCKHOLM • ATHENS • TOKYO • MILAN
MADRID • WARSAW • BUDAPEST • AUCKLAND

ISBN 0-373-17162-5

BAY OF RAINBOWS

Copyright © 1993 by Dana James.

CHAPTER ONE

OUTSIDE in the April sunshine the temperature was over seventy degrees, but Polly felt chilled as she looked with rising desperation towards the window. Out there lay freedom.

In the streaked and dusty glass she glimpsed her reflection and saw a drawn elfin face and green eyes huge with anxiety. Her dark curly hair, cut short for convenience rather than fashion, clung like damp feathers to her forehead and temples. This couldn't be happening. Not to her.

Gleaming like a huge silver bird, a passenger jet approached the runway which pointed like a finger out into the sparkling sapphire waters of Gibraltar Bay. Engines roaring, it swooped in to land, braking hard as its wheels touched the wide runway which was crossed halfway along by the single road connecting the British colony to the Spanish mainland.

This was the fourth plane Polly had heard arrive since she had been literally dragged from the boat, marched along the marina, and bundled into the white-painted Customs building.

'Try to see the situation from my point of view, Miss Levington.' On the far side of the desk the shirt-sleeved Customs officer leaned back in his chair and lit a cigarette, blowing a thin plume of smoke towards the cracked and yellowing ceiling.

Stockily built, with unshockable brown eyes and black hair liberally laced with grey, he spoke in a tone

5

of weary cynicism. 'Do you seriously expect me to believe you knew nothing about it?'

His colleague, sitting on the far side of the room taking written notes of the questions and answers, looked up as he too waited for her answer.

Polly stiffened her spine. 'Yes, I can,' she retorted crisply. 'Because that's the truth.'

'Mr Kemp didn't tell you what was in the box?'

'Yes, he did. He said it contained engine components. That's what was on the label. I had no reason to believe it was anything else.'

'You didn't think it strange that he would be prepared to go to Marseilles to deliver these engine parts? After all, your destination was the Greek islands. That's quite a detour.'

Polly shrugged. 'I did wonder. But Clive—Mr Kemp—said it was a rule of the sea to help another boat in distress. Besides, he was sure we'd quickly make up the time once we got out to sea. Look, you've asked me these questions several times already. What else can I say? I've told you the truth, exactly as it happened. I'll admit I may have been naïve. . . '

They both knew that was the understatement of the decade, though her small, defiantly tilted chin challenged him to say so out loud. 'But that's hardly a crime.'

The Customs officer's eyes narrowed. 'No. However, smuggling heroin most definitely is.'

'But I *wouldn't*—I *didn't*——' Polly cried, then broke off, fastening her lower lip between her teeth to stop herself venting her frustration and growing fear on the man opposite. He was only doing his job. It was Clive who had got her into this mess. The next time she saw him, she would give him such a tongue-lashing that his ears would ring for a week!

But when would she see him? Where was he? They had been hustled off the boat separately, and her inquisitor had simply ignored her demands to have Clive brought in so that he could confirm she had had no knowledge of what was going on. Instead he had relentlessly bombarded her with the same questions.

Polly took a deep breath, proud of the way her voice emerged, calm and steady, even though her heartbeat thundered in her ears. 'If you think this constant repetition will force me to confess to something I didn't do, you couldn't be more wrong. I've told you everything I know.'

She deliberately turned her head to gaze out of the window once more. Clive Kemp's suggestion that she join him on a cruise across the Mediterranean had seemed the perfect antidote to a long hard winter, a series of temping jobs which had been more demanding than usual, and the unpleasantness of her break-up with Giles.

The trip had also offered temporary escape from her mother's pointed reminiscences that when she was Polly's age she had already been married two years and was preparing for the birth of her first child.

But what had started out as a dream come true had, within hours of their leaving England, turned into a nightmare.

'Ask Clive,' Polly repeated for what felt like the hundredth time. 'He'll confirm everything I've said.'

The Customs officer tilted his head to one side, observing her through eyes slitted against the smoke. 'Ask him to incriminate himself? Is it likely he'll do that, Miss Levington?' he enquired reasonably.

She gritted her teeth. 'He'll have to. Because what I've told you is the truth.'

A telephone on the wide, scarred desk buzzed.

Lifting the receiver, the Customs officer drew heavily on his cigarette. 'He has arrived? I'll come at once.' He hung up.

'Is that Clive?' Polly asked quickly. She might as well have saved her breath. And from the sudden change in her inquisitor's manner, she realised that it couldn't possibly be. Clive Kemp was not the kind of man to inspire such respectful, obedient haste.

Crushing the cigarette stub in an overflowing ash-tray, the officer pushed his chair back and stood up. 'Please excuse me.'

'How much longer do you intend to keep me here?' Polly pleaded. 'Surely I have a right to know that at least?'

Reaching the door, he paused and turned. 'Perhaps you would like a cup of coffee. I will have one sent in.' Glancing at his colleague, he made a brief movement with his head, indicating that he too should leave.

The door closed behind them and Polly was left alone once more.

She bit her lip, fighting the fear that threatened to overwhelm her. Why had they rushed off like that? Why wouldn't the officer in charge tell her what was happening? *Who* had arrived? Did it have anything to do with her being held here? *What was going on*?

She had told him over and over again the sequence of events on the boat. He had been consistently polite, but he didn't believe her.

She had not been intimidated or threatened in any way. But nor had she been allowed to use the tele-phone or leave the office, except for one visit to the toilet down the corridor accompanied by a sour-faced secretary who weighed at least twelve stone and insisted she leave the door ajar.

She was completely innocent, but how could she

prove it? Clive could clear her, but would he? And would they believe *him*?

She shuddered, and the knot in her stomach tightened.

The first time Clive had mentioned the trip she had laughed, thinking he was kidding. But he had insisted the invitation was genuine.

What finally decided her to accept was his ready agreement to her one condition, that a shipboard romance was definitely off limits. Having just painfully disentangled herself from one relationship, she had no intention of getting involved in another for a very long time.

Another thought surfaced from the chaos in her mind—and stuck, looming larger and more unnerving by the moment. No one outside this building knew she was here. There was no one ringing lawyers on her behalf, no one working to get her out. No one to stop them keeping her here for as long as they wanted.

Polly's skin crawled and she shivered violently. She hated this feeling of helplessness, of no longer being in control of her own life.

Standing up, she walked from one side of the window to the other, her movements stiff and her legs trembly from the accumulated tension in her muscles.

When she and Clive had arrived that morning, the air had been crystal-clear, the view razor-sharp, colours vivid and bright. But now, the lowering sun was a huge orange ball and across the bay the hills behind Algeciras were purple-shadowed.

What would happen next? Would they put her in a cell for the night? Her mind sheered away from images she didn't want to dwell on.

She hadn't been allowed to bring anything off the boat except her patchwork leather shoulder-bag which had been thoroughly searched first. One of the officers had advised her to take a sweater. With the temperature touching seventy, twenty degrees higher than in London, it had seemed a ridiculous suggestion. But, too shaken by what was happening to argue, she had picked up her Aran cardigan.

Clive had insisted she wear it, together with a waterproof jacket, on the flight over. But his warning that Mediterranean springs were dangerously unpredictable was evidently just one more lie among all the others he had told her.

Turning from the window, Polly picked her bag up and opened it on the desk. It no longer contained her passport, which the Customs officer had immediately confiscated. Pushing aside her purse and the wallet of traveller's cheques, she took out a comb, a packet of moist clean-up squares and a wad of tissues.

Her self-confidence might have taken a battering, but that was no reason to forfeit the personal standards her parents had instilled into her since childhood.

As she wiped her face with one of the astringent-soaked squares, Polly's hand grew still. Her parents. How would they react when the news reached them?

'Sure you know what you're doing, Poll?' Her father had eyed her over his gold-rimmed half-glasses. He hadn't been seriously doubtful. He trusted her judgement. He was simply checking that she had considered all the angles before reaching her decision to go.

And she had. She was a strong swimmer, a good cook, and she had received Clive's assurance that their relationship would remain strictly platonic. All likely problem areas had been covered.

How could she possibly have foreseen a situation like this?

While accepting that the trip was a once-in-a-lifetime

opportunity, her mother had been less happy about it. However, as her dearest wish was for Polly to follow her two sisters' example and 'settle down', that was not surprising.

But I'm *not* my sisters. Polly dried her face. Feeling much refreshed, she crumpled the tissues with the empty packet into a tight ball and tossed the lot into the waste basket. I'm *me*. And I want to live my own life my own way.

Well, you've certainly got off to a cracking start, mocked a small ironic voice inside her.

Raking the comb through cropped curls that gleamed like polished mahogany, Polly tried to stifle her doubts and the nagging feeling that somehow she should have known there would be strings attached to Clive's offer no matter how much he protested otherwise.

Behind her the door opened. She glanced round, expecting to see the secretary with her promised cup of coffee.

Towering head and shoulders above the Customs officer, who stood aside to let him pass, the man strode in, his face as dark and threatening as an impending storm.

Polly jerked as though she had been slapped. With every nerve tingling she lowered her hand, barely feeling the comb bite into her palm as her grip tightened.

As their eyes met, his narrowed fractionally. But the impression that he had been caught off guard was so fleeting that Polly was sure she must have imagined it.

The Customs officer closed the door softly, almost reverently, leaving her and the newcomer alone.

She had recognised him instantly, though she had

seen him in the flesh only once before and that had been across a crowded ballroom.

As usual he had been accompanied by a beautiful woman. Her arm linked through his, publicly staking her claim, the woman had gazed adoringly up at him, and with ill-concealed triumph at everyone else.

Was *he* the cause of all that fuss on the phone?

'Good evening.' Though deep and resonant, the man's voice had a chilling softness. His blue-grey eyes were as cold as a Siberian winter, and Polly felt as though she had been impaled by twin icicles.

His head lifted fractionally, his nostrils flaring, and she knew he had scented the astringent lotion.

'For someone who's just attempted something incredibly stupid, you've got nerve, I will say that,' he observed, his gaze flickering to the comb in her white-knuckled fingers.

Polly thrust it back into her bag, embarrassed at being caught doing things more properly done in a ladies' cloakroom, and furious at her own embarrassment. It wasn't vanity that had prompted her to freshen herself up. She was clinging desperately to normality and self-respect.

His eyes returned, colder than ever, to meet hers. 'Or perhaps you simply lack the intelligence or imagination to recognise just how much trouble you're in.'

Dumbstruck at this insult, Polly could only stare at him.

The newcomer moved behind the desk as if he had every right simply to walk in and take over. And as he pushed aside some papers to make room for his briefcase he did indeed exude a powerful air of authority.

Taking out a sheaf of documents, he laid them on the desk top. 'Right, let's see what can be salvaged from this mess.' He glanced up. 'By the way, my name is——'

'I know who you are, Mr Bryce.' Polly found her tongue at last and spoke with all the frosty dignity she could muster. 'What I don't understand is what you're doing here, or why you find it necessary to be so rude.'

If he expected her to fawn the way the Customs officer had done he was going to be disappointed. Hell would freeze first!

His eyes narrowed again. 'Where have I seen you before?'

Trying to pretend he had mistaken her for someone else was obviously not going to work. In any case, Polly remembered the occasion all too clearly.

'We happened to be in the same place at the same time a couple of months ago,' she replied, terse and offhand. But inside she was cringing at the memory of that appalling evening at the Grand Hotel.

She hadn't wanted to go at all. But the company she was temping for was a subsidiary of Bryce International and her boss had left her in no doubt that *everyone* was expected to attend. Which meant Giles would be there.

The terrible things he'd said still haunted her: He had used words as weapons to slash and destroy her self-esteem. Every time she imagined coming face to face with him her stomach knotted. She had tried desperately to think of a reason for not going which her boss would accept. There wasn't one.

Knowing nothing of her problems with Giles, the other girls in the office hadn't been able to understand her reluctance.

Their anticipation had been at fever pitch for days. Discussions about what they should wear had been interspersed with sexy gossip concerning the star of the occasion, Nathan Bryce.

Against her will Polly had found herself curious about the subject of such intense speculation. Of course she had heard of him—it was impossible for anyone interested in sailing *not* to know who he was. And she had seen his picture in trade papers and yachting magazines, usually alongside an article extolling his brilliance, not only as a prizewinning designer in the highly competitive world of trans-ocean racing, but also as a respected if demanding skipper.

Though her practical knowledge of sailing was nonexistent she loved reading about boats and watching them race. And her one trip across the bay on a six-berth Swedish cruiser-racer owned by a visiting friend of her father's was a treasured memory.

As he mounted the dais to receive his award, Nathan Bryce had been taller than she expected, and startlingly handsome in a beautifully tailored suit. The crisp white shirt was a stark contrast to his weatherbeaten tan and dark hair that curled, thick and in need of a cut, on his collar.

There was something about him that set him apart from the other men in the room. He radiated power, yet he wasn't loud. His gestures were brief and controlled. His humour was dry and delivered deadpan. Yet such was the force of his personality that every eye was fixed on him. Even the sound of a pin dropping would have been a gross intrusion.

As flashbulbs popped and he paid tribute to everyone involved in building the sleek yacht which had won the award his eyes roamed the room.

Just for a second it seemed to Polly that they met and lingered on hers. But at that same moment Giles had lurched through the crowd to her side and draped a possessive arm around her shoulders, muttering through a cloud of whisky fumes that they had to talk.

Recoiling, Polly twisted away from him. 'There's nothing to talk about, Giles.' She managed to keep her voice quiet and level, though every nerve was screaming. 'You said it all. Our. . .relationship, such as it was, is over, finished.'

He gripped her arm. 'Listen, I——'

She pulled free. 'Please, Giles, don't.' She could feel her colour mounting and sensed nudges and stares.

He glared at her for a moment, his small eyes hot with a weak man's rage. Then his face crumpled in anguish. 'You took what you could get and now you're moving on, is that it?' he demanded, making no effort to lower his voice. He looked and sounded ready to burst into tears.

She was too stunned to move. She couldn't believe he was actually doing this.

'I suppose you've already got your eye on some other poor sucker. Men have a name for girls like you, and it's not flattering——'

Alerted to the commotion, one of the stewards arrived and gently but firmly piloted Giles away.

Heart pounding as she burned with embarrassment, Polly saw Giles glance back over his shoulder and *wink*.

The night they parted after that last dreadful row, he had sworn he would get even. This deliberate and cruel humiliation was his revenge.

Her throat stiff with tears of rage, Polly bit the inside of her lip so hard that she tasted the warm saltiness of blood. She would not cry. She would not give him the satisfaction.

But only stubborn pride and the knowledge that Giles's monstrous accusations were totally unfounded prevented her from fleeing to the Ladies'.

Trying desperately to ignore the rustle of whispers around her, Polly focused her gaze on Nathan Bryce. But though he resumed his speech as though the interruption had never happened, his gaze, holding hers for a moment longer, had turned cold and cynical.

It was as though he had slapped her. It didn't make sense. He was a complete stranger, of no importance to her whatever. Yet that brief derisive stare pierced her to her soul. He had accused, judged, and branded her all in the space of a few seconds. The monstrous injustice of it took her breath away.

The instant he finished, Polly slipped through the applauding crowd, grabbed her coat from the cloakroom, and took a taxi home.

The memory faded and her eyes refocused on the nicotine-yellowed wall of the Customs office. She glanced up at him, swallowing. 'I attended a party at which you were the guest of honour.'

'Ah, yes, I remember now.' He eyed her coolly. 'Didn't running away afterwards rather defeat the object?'

Polly stared at him, totally confused. 'What object? What do you mean?'

'Such innocence.' Though a mocking smile played at the corners of his chiselled mouth, his voice had a caustic bite. 'Still, as a means of attracting my attention that scene had a certain novelty.'

Her eyes widened. 'Surely you don't think—you *can't* believe I——' She broke off, incoherent with anger. 'How dare you?' she choked. 'That *scene* was not of my making. It was horrible. I——' She bent her head, shaking it quickly as she fought off tears.

Then fury at his assumption overwhelmed her again. 'I didn't even want to *be* at the presentation. That's no reflection on your professional achievements,' she added quickly. 'You deserved the award.' As his brows climbed sardonically she cursed her sense of fairness. He would only see it as a weakness to be used against her, or worse, as an attempt to ingratiate herself.

'But if you think I'd make a public exhibition of myself to catch *any* man's attention, you don't know *me* at all.' Her face burned with indignation. Handsome, talented, and wealthy he might be, but he was also rude and abrasive, and she had done nothing to deserve such treatment.

Yearning for a drink to ease her parched throat, Polly moistened her lips with the tip of her tongue. 'Mr Bryce, I don't know you. I don't particularly *want* to know you.'

Not now she didn't. But when their eyes had met across the packed ballroom, for a fleeting instant the crowd had ceased to exist. There had been only him, only her, and she had wondered. But it had been just a momentary longing for something she seemed destined never to have. She must have been mad to consider the possibility, especially after the emotional battering she had received from Giles.

In any case, she was completely different from the generously curved blondes Nathan Bryce was usually seen with. Like the one he was with that night. His apparent interest could not possibly have been more than passing curiosity. And that had swiftly turned to censure and contempt.

Polly stiffened her spine. 'We have absolutely nothing in common, Mr Bryce. And I can't even begin to imagine why you're here.'

He had been watching her without a flicker of expression. The glitter in his hooded eyes made it impossible for her to hazard even the wildest guess at what he was thinking. So why did she have this totally irrational feeling that she had surprised him?

She wished he wouldn't look at her like that. It was making her heartbeat erratic, and her whole body had broken out in a fine dew of perspiration.

'As the boat you were using for your ridiculous smuggling attempt belongs to me I should have thought it was obvious.'

Polly stiffened. 'What are you talking about? *Seawitch* isn't yours.'

'She most certainly is,' he retorted icily. 'I designed her, I built her, and she's registered in my name.' He raised the sheaf of papers. 'And as, thanks to you and Mr Kemp, she is presently under guard in the marina, naturally I've brought all the relevant documents to prove that.' His dark brows rose. 'Surely even you couldn't imagine I'd claim ownership without the proof to back it up?'

'But I thought——' She broke off abruptly. This was something else Clive had been less than truthful about. To be fair, she couldn't recall actually hearing him say the boat was his, but he certainly hadn't corrected her when she had assumed him to be the owner.

Belatedly the insinuation beneath his cutting sarcasm registered. Her chin came up. 'What do you mean, *even* me?' she demanded.

'Someone of your obviously limited intelligence,' he said coldly.

Polly flinched. The chill of fear and loneliness that had penetrated her very bones was suddenly consumed by the fury that engulfed her like a wave. Her entire body flamed with a rage that banished her nervousness and freed her tongue from all restraint.

'I see. Without giving me a chance to explain you've

decided that not only am I guilty, but I'm a moron as well.' She looked him up and down in open disgust. 'So much for good old British justice! Whatever happened to the concept that a person is innocent until proved guilty?'

'*Innocent*?' His expression was contemptuous. 'Miss Levington, you were caught on *my* boat with enough heroin to——'

'Stop right there!' Polly cried. '*I* was not caught with anything. I told the Customs officers and now I'm telling you—I knew nothing about the heroin.'

His face darkened with anger. 'Don't insult my intelligence!'

'Why not?' She threw the words at him. 'You're insulting mine.' She flung her hands up in a gesture that combined defiance and despair. 'I didn't know Clive had stolen your wretched boat. And I didn't know about the drugs until the Customs launch stopped us in the bay. But as you can't or won't recognise the truth even when it's told you, there's really no point in continuing this conversation.'

She turned her back on him and stared blindly out of the window. 'Perhaps on your way out you'd ask about the coffee I was promised.' Her voice trembled, but she steadied it quickly. 'I haven't eaten since breakfast, and that was in London.'

'If that's a bid for sympathy,' Nathan Bryce said grimly, 'you're wasting your time.'

Polly whirled to face him, flinching at the derision that had hardened his features. How dared he look at her like that? She hadn't *done* anything.

She drew herself up. 'It's a statement of fact,' she said, adding with quiet dignity, 'I don't want sympathy, Mr Bryce. I want justice. Is that too much to ask?'

The change in his expression was barely perceptible.

But it was as if, for the first time, he was seeing beyond the image his assumptions had created.

His gaze met and held hers. The drab cheerless office, the charges she was facing, Clive's betrayal, all faded into oblivion.

An invisible lightning leaped between them. Nathan Bryce's mask of disdain cracked and Polly glimpsed shock. He turned away, deliberately breaking the contact.

She felt breathless and shaky and *terrified*. No. Not him.

'How old are you?' he demanded. There was a slight hoarseness in his voice which she hadn't noticed before.

She winced, smarting beneath memories of Giles's disbelief and the greedy delight that had turned to frustrated irritation. Virginity at her age was a positive handicap, he had insisted. A condition to be rectified as quickly as possible if she didn't want to be labelled a freak, or worse.

Polly bit her lip. Her time with Giles had cost her the equivalent of a layer of skin. Emotional bruises didn't show, but they left a painful vulnerability which she hated.

'My age is irrelevant, and none of your business.'

His brows rose at this flash of spirit. 'I disagree,' he said softly. 'A headstrong and impressionable eighteen-year-old looking for adventure might possibly win some sympathy from a judge with daughters of his own. On the other hand,' the flat menace in his voice silenced her indignant denial before it could be voiced, 'a woman in her twenties might reasonably be expected to show more intelligence. But you're not obliged to answer. I can always check your passport.'

Flushed and furious, Polly gasped, 'You have no right——'

'Don't you dare quote *rights* at me, young woman,' he snarled. 'It was *my* boat you were caught on, remember? How do you suppose that reflects on me?' His eyes burned like cold blue flames and Polly wondered if that moment of soul-searing contact had simply been a cruel trick of her imagination.

'My heart bleeds for you,' she blazed back. Never in her whole life had she met anyone so *self*-centred. 'It's terrible to be accused of something you haven't done. How will it affect your family? What will your friends and colleagues say? How do you prove you had nothing to do with it, especially when certain people are determined to believe you did?' She paused for breath, her heart thudding painfully against her ribs.

'I know exactly how you feel, because I'm as innocent in this as you are. I didn't know about the drugs.'

He was her only link with the outside world, the key to her freedom. She *had* to convince him.

There was a knock on the door and the senior Customs officer leaned in.

Turning their backs on her, the two men talked in whispers. Nathan seemed to be asking questions. Then the officer withdrew once more.

Fear wrapped icy tentacles around Polly's heart. 'What is it? What does he want?'

'You,' came the succinct reply. 'Get your things together.'

Hope flared wildly. 'Are they letting me go?'

Nathan shook his head, his mouth twisting in a humourless smile. 'Hardly.' Gathering up the papers, he replaced them in his briefcase.

Polly swallowed. 'Then what——?'

His face expressionless, Nathan glanced across at her. 'You're going to be charged.'

CHAPTER TWO

POLLY felt the blood drain from her face. She tried to speak, but her lips were numb. The room rocked slowly around her.

'Sit down,' Nathan ordered.

She stared at him. She knew he had spoken, she had watched his mouth move. But she hadn't been able to hear what he said for the roaring in her ears.

Striding quickly round the desk, he grasped her arm. His touch on her bare skin seared like a brand. 'Sit down,' he repeated, guiding her to a chair. The moment she was seated he let her go, but she could still feel the imprint of his grip like iron wrapped in velvet. 'You look pale, and I don't want you passing out on me before I've heard the rest of this story.'

'How kind,' she muttered. But the spark of rebellion was quickly extinguished by relief. Her legs felt like foam rubber. Had she not taken her weight off them they would simply have given way.

Sprawling at his feet would not have done much for her dignity. And doubtless his reaction would have been to enquire coolly whether this was another bid for sympathy.

Nathan returned to his own side of the desk and sat down. Leaning forward, he rested his bronzed forearms on the scarred surface and toyed with a pen. 'Now,' he demanded softly, 'what were you doing on board *Seawitch*?'

Polly took a deep breath and passed a shaking hand

across her clammy forehead. Once the fog cleared from her brain she'd be fine.

'Clive told me he was taking his boat——'

'*His* boat?' Nathan interrupted. 'He said *Seawitch* was his?'

Polly's face puckered as she tried to remember. 'Yes—no——' Her gesture of hopelessness mirrored her confusion. 'I'm not sure. But he certainly gave me the impression the boat belonged to him.'

'How did you meet him?' The words sprayed at her like bullets.

'You missed your vocation, Mr Bryce.' Polly licked paper-dry lips. 'Being chief interrogator in some tinpot little dictatorship would have suited you perfectly.'

'Kindly answer the question, Miss Levington,' he replied. Though his features looked as if they'd been carved from stone, in the depths of his gaze something stirred. Amusement? Respect? But it was quickly gone.

She swallowed. 'I'm a temporary secretary. My last job was at Mediterranean Charters. Clive works for them as a delivery skipper. He takes yachts from wherever they've been laid up for the winter to their summer cruising grounds.'

'I know what a delivery skipper does, Miss Levington,' Nathan Bryce said curtly. 'What I *still* don't know is what you were doing on board my boat.'

'Maybe I could tell you if you didn't keep interrupting,' Polly cried, feeling her stomach clench as his mouth tightened and he turned the full power of his steely gaze on her. 'Clive told me he was sailing to the Greek islands and invited me to go with him.'

One corner of Nathan's mouth lifted in derision. 'And you accepted. Just like that.' His smile was oddly bitter.

The implication was all too plain, and Polly felt herself flush. 'It wasn't like *that* at all,' she protested hotly. 'I was to work my passage.' Hot colour flamed her cheeks as his brows rose in sardonic query. 'As a cook,' she added tersely, making no attempt to hide her disgust at his silent insinuation. 'And I paid my own flight out.'

'That was very independent of you,' he remarked. 'So your relationship with Mr Kemp——'

'There was—is—no relationship between Clive and me,' Polly said fiercely. 'I didn't even know him all that well.'

'Really?' Nathan's scepticism flicked across her raw nerves like a whiplash. 'Yet you were prepared to sail almost two thousand miles to the Greek islands with him.'

'Why not?' she demanded. 'My interest in him was confined to his seamanship. As a yacht delivery skipper he had to be a damn good sailor. He was offering me the trip of a lifetime, and all I had to do was take care of the meals. It seemed like a fair deal.'

She tilted her small chin defiantly. 'I think it's high time you stopped making snap judgements, Mr Bryce, especially as the conclusions you leap to are invariably the wrong ones.'

'Tell me, Miss Levington,' he enquired with silky smoothness, 'as you're such an expert on human nature, why did Giles Denton make a point of publicly embarrassing you at the Grand Hotel?'

Polly gulped. 'You know Giles?'

'I know his reputation,' he corrected coldly.

'I, unfortunately, did not,' she murmured, her wounded smile a brief spasm mocking her own gullibility.

Memories of that evening were still painfully vivid.

Not just Giles's spite-filled revenge, but the expression in Nathan Bryce's eyes as he had gazed down from the dais. It was that cold contempt, the same icy disdain with which he was observing her now, which had prompted her to try and set the record straight.

'Yet you were with him at the presentation.'

'I was not *with* him,' Polly responded angrily.

'Really?' His tone was cutting and his lips twisted in a cynical sneer. 'Yet of all the women present it was you whose shoulder Denton put his arm around, and your ear he was whispering in.'

'I didn't invite that,' Polly cried. 'He'd been drinking.'

'For Dutch courage? Or was he drowning his sorrows?'

She clenched her fists. But even as she drew breath to hurl a furious retort at him, something clicked in her brain.

He was *trying* to provoke her, deliberately goading her into saying more than she intended.

She saw his eyes change and knew he had witnessed her realisation. Beneath her anger she was afraid. Something was happening between her and this man that she didn't understand.

Her tongue flicked out to moisten her lips. 'I don't think my private life is any of your business, Mr Bryce.'

'You don't?' His voice was as soft and rich as black velvet and his hooded gaze held her captive. 'First you're involved in a fracas with a man at a party held in *my* honour. Then you turn up, with a different man, accused of smuggling drugs on *my* boat.'

His smile was terrifying. 'I'd say your private life is very much my business. And you've *made* it so.'

'But——'

'How odd that you didn't immediately see through a phony like Giles Denton,' he grated, totally ignoring her interruption, 'and after agreeing to take a cruise with a man you admit you hardly know, you end up in custody accused of drug-smuggling. What an amazing sense of judgement that shows.'

She shrivelled in the icy blast of his scorn.

'You, Miss Levington,' his mouth curled, 'are a mobile disaster area, an accident looking for a place to happen.'

Polly swallowed. She must have been mad to try to appeal to his better nature. He didn't have one.

Turning her back on him, she stared out of the window. The sun trembled for an instant on the edge of the distant hills, then started to sink behind them. The wind had dropped and everything was still, poised in that limbo between day and evening.

'I don't deserve this,' she whispered. She wanted desperately to make him understand that she wasn't the kind of girl Giles had labelled her. Just for an instant she wondered why it mattered to her what Nathan Bryce thought. Because I'm innocent, she told herself fiercely. But underneath there was another reason, one she didn't dare look at too closely.

'Life isn't necessarily fair, Miss Levington,' he rapped. 'The fact that *my* boat was used in this smuggling attempt is going to take some living down.'

'It hasn't done my reputation a whole lot of good either,' Polly blazed at him. Tears of fury and frustration blurred her vision, and she blinked them away. 'It's not a pleasant feeling to find out you've been taken for a ride by someone you trusted.'

Nathan regarded her without speaking. His face was totally devoid of expression, but the intensity of his gaze told her his mind was working with the speed and emotionless precision of a computer.

Polly looked away, shivering as despair gnawed at the edges of her mind. There was nothing more she could say or do to prove that what she had told him was the truth. It was up to him. Either he believed her or he didn't.

The door opened again and the Customs officer leaned in, nodded once at Nathan, and withdrew. But this time he left the door open.

Nathan stood up. Even in faded jeans and a lemon T-shirt he was still the most imposing, *unnerving* man Polly had ever met.

'Right,' he said briskly, 'time to go.' His face was set, making it impossible for her to guess what was going on in his mind.

'Go? Where?' she asked nervously.

A brief impatience tightened his features. 'To the police station.'

'Don't you believe me?' she croaked, her throat dry with apprehension as she stood up. He legs still felt slightly wobbly.

Tucking his briefcase under his arm, Nathan opened the door, glancing over his shoulder at her. 'You're asking *me* for a snap judgement, Miss Levington?' His cool irony brought swift colour to her cheeks as she recalled how furiously she had condemned him for doing just that.

Before she could ask any more questions she was ushered outside into a waiting car. As Nathan got in beside her, the Customs officer who had questioned her slid into the front passenger-seat.

The car sped noisily away from the marina and into the narrow streets of the town. Polly clutched her bag and cardigan, her mind teeming with questions she was afraid to ask. Nathan's silence made him remote and even more intimidating.

It was infuriating that she should need this arrogant cynic who only had to snap his fingers for the world to leap to attention, anxious to please. Yet she was relying on this very power to get her released. He might be the key to her freedom, but she still hated him for the confusion he aroused in her.

Though she was huddled in the corner as far from him as she could get, the car wasn't very big, and every time they went round a corner his thigh and shoulder pressed against hers. Despite all her efforts to ignore it the sensation lingered on to torment her long after the contact had been broken.

They arrived at the police station, and for Polly the next half-hour was a blur. She was led into an office not unlike the one she had recently left, and charges were read out. Seated at one side of the room, she watched while Nathan held quiet discussions with a policeman and the Customs officer on the far side.

She felt strangely detached. She knew it was her they were talking about, but the shock of her arrest, the exhausting interview with Nathan Bryce, lack of food and the unaccustomed heat had totally drained her.

Someone brought her a coffee and she smiled vague thanks, noting with the same odd detachment that her hands were shaking as she clasped them around the mug.

She sipped and swallowed, trying to keep her mind blank as the coffee curled, hot and strong, in her stomach. But Nathan Bryce kept invading her thoughts. It wasn't that she *wanted* to think about him, but he was as easy to ignore as an earthquake.

Another man was respectfully ushered in and introduced to Nathan. He wore a formal suit and had the pressured air of someone who had been side-tracked from an important engagement. The two men shook hands and yet more intensive talks followed.

As the coffee revived her she began to catch odd words and phrases. 'As a magistrate. . .formal application. . .prosecutor might oppose. . .gravity of the offence. . .likelihood of defendant absconding. . . interference with investigations. . .'

She could see Nathan arguing with quiet forcefulness and sensed some hard bargaining in progress. She didn't like him, but hoped desperately that he would win. It was strange and horribly unsettling to have such violently opposing feelings about a person.

The Customs officer, policeman, and magistrate began to nod, at first uncertain, reluctant, then with growing accord. With handshakes all round everyone left, leaving her and Nathan alone.

He was standing with his back to her. She watched him raise one hand to rub the nape of his neck, then flex his shoulder muscles.

Her detachment was rapidly being replaced by nervousness. It was *her* fate these men had been deciding. And obviously a decision had been reached. She wanted to know, and yet was terrified of what he might tell her.

He turned, the swift movement making her jump. Though his expression gave nothing away a muscle flickered at the point of his jaw. Polly found it strangely reassuring. It showed that beneath the granite exterior emotion did exist, even if it was struggling for survival.

'I've managed to get you released on bail.'

Polly gazed at him, not knowing whether to laugh or cry. He was telling her the cage door was open but she was still chained to the bars. She struggled to keep her voice level. 'I've—I've only got a hundred pounds in traveller's cheques. I don't suppose that will be anything like enough.'

He brushed her words aside. 'I've put up the money.'

Her eyes widened in stunned surprise. '*You* have?'

'Well, you're not much use to anyone in here.'

Polly took his laconic retort to mean that the police and Customs officers would be glad to have her off their hands. Shaken as she was by his startlingly generous gesture, and weak with relief, it didn't occur to her that his words, or his actions, might be open to a different interpretation.

She scanned the drab office with its scarred furniture, scuffed paintwork and nicotine-yellowed ceiling.

'I can't wait to get out of this place,' she breathed. It wasn't easy to be grateful to Nathan Bryce. He was ruthless, impatient, and, though in public he seemed self-effacing, he was only too aware of his power and the impact he had on people.

On the other hand, it was due entirely to his efforts that she wouldn't be spending her first night in Gibraltar in a prison cell.

She raised her head, met his piercing gaze, and smiled. 'Thank you. I really do appreciate what you've done.' Her smile faltered. Why was he looking at her so strangely?

'You should do that more often,' he said, his own expression oddly guarded.

'Do what?'

'Smile.'

She pulled a wry face. 'I don't seem to have had a lot to smile about just lately. And today hasn't exactly been a barrel of laughs. For either of us,' she acknowledged.

Picking up her bag, she slung the strap over her shoulder. He probably wanted to get the formalities over so he could be on his way. Well, she certainly didn't intend to hold him up.

'If you'd like to give me a paper to sign saying how much I owe you,' she said briskly, 'the moment I get home I'll make arrangements to have the money paid into your account.'

Raising the cash wasn't going to be easy. She knew her father would lend her whatever she needed to cancel her debt to Nathan Bryce, but she couldn't ask him. After paying for her younger sister's lavish wedding last autumn he had begun saving for the world cruise he had promised her mother for their thirtieth wedding anniversary. Though it was still several months off they were both getting excited, planning their itinerary, and making lists of the clothes they would need.

In any case, it would be too awful having to explain *why* she needed it. What a mockery that would make of her insistence that she was independent and perfectly able to take care of herself.

No, she definitely couldn't ask him. She would have to find some way of raising the money herself. She had said she would pay it back and she would keep her word, even if it meant scrubbing floors and washing dishes. After all, it surely couldn't be *that* much.

There was a strange light in Nathan's eyes. 'That will not be necessary,' he told her.

Though his expression was enigmatic, Polly sensed he was laughing at her. Angry, humiliated, she stiffened.

'Look, Mr Bryce, I'm very grateful for what you've

done. Lord knows how long I'd have been stuck in here before they finally realised I was telling the truth. But I'm not remaining in your debt one second longer than I have to. As soon as I've collected my things from the boat I'll catch the first plane home and——'

'No,' Nathan cut her short, 'I'm afraid that won't be possible.'

Bewildered, her unease growing by the moment, Polly lifted her chin. 'Why not?' she demanded.

His brows rose. 'Because I need you here.'

His impatient reply made her hackles rise even as a tiny treacherous thrill slithered along her veins. Nathan Bryce needed *her*?

She frowned, hugging her bag close in an unconscious gesture of self-protection. 'What on earth for?'

'It's perfectly simple. *Seawitch* has to be at her berth in Kalamaki marina by the fourth of May.'

Polly frowned. 'I don't understand. Why the hurry?'

'A change of plan,' Nathan said tersely. 'Circumstances outside my control.'

She shrugged. She couldn't see what he was getting at. 'That has nothing to do with me.'

'Oh, but it does,' he said with that deadly softness that sent shivers rippling down her spine. 'Because I'll have to sail her there myself.'

She gazed at him blankly. 'So?'

He sighed, clearly exasperated that something so obvious should require explanation. 'I don't want to make the voyage single-handed. I need a crew. Someone who can cook.'

Polly felt the blood drain from her face. She shook her head so hard she felt dizzy.

'Besides,' he continued, completely ignoring her silent refusal, 'keeping this case's star witness out of sight until the trial will help avoid any bad publicity.'

She stared at him. She could hardly believe it. After all, why should he care? 'You'd do that for *me*?'

His dark brows rose and his mouth curled cynically. 'It's *my* reputation I'm concerned for, Miss Levington. *Seawitch* is my boat, and that implicates me. Any association with drug running, no matter how unfounded, could cause considerable harm to my business.' His expression hardened. 'That's something I will not tolerate. So, you sail with me.'

'No. Absolutely not.' It wasn't until after she had spoken that she realised how violently she had reacted, and it shook her.

All right, she could see his point. Moving *Seawitch* and herself out of Gibraltar would be the quickest and most effective way of killing public interest. But while a cruise across the Mediterranean with Clive Kemp had posed no problems at all, the very thought of being alone on a boat with Nathan Bryce for however long it took to sail two thousand miles brought her out in a cold sweat and turned her insides to jelly. 'It's out of the question,' she repeated.

The silence vibrated with tension, and Polly felt her nerves stretch almost to snapping point.

Nathan looked down at her for a moment, then inclined his head, the movement brief and dismissive. 'As you wish.' He picked up his briefcase, resting it on the desk. 'I must have misunderstood. I thought you were anxious to get out of here.'

'You know I am.' Fear was an acrid taste in Polly's mouth as she gazed at him. She swallowed hard. 'Look, if this is your idea of a joke, I don't find it at all funny.'

'I never joke about money, Miss Levington.' He opened the flap to check briefly inside. 'And there's a very great deal of money at stake here.'

Polly's throat was uncomfortably dry. 'Exactly how much *is* my bail?'

'Twenty-five thousand.'

Her hand flew to her throat. '*How* much?' she croaked.

Nathan moved one shoulder in a semi-shrug. 'They take drug-smuggling very seriously here. But that's peanuts compared with what I stand to lose if I don't get *Seawitch* to Athens by the fourth.'

'Why?' Her curiosity got the better of her. She couldn't prevent the question slipping out. 'What's in Athens that's so important?'

'Not what,' he corrected, 'who.' Pushing his briefcase aside, he lowered himself into a chair, rested his elbow on the back, and crossed one leg over the other. 'Sit down, Miss Levington.'

As she hesitated he nodded towards the chair next to his. It was obvious he had no intention of saying anything more until she obeyed.

Inwardly fuming, Polly compressed her lips and sat down, still clasping her bag tightly.

'That's better,' Nathan smiled, his eyes hooded and unreadable. 'First let me explain why I have to go to Athens. I've designed a new yacht which we believe stands an excellent chance of winning the next round-the-world race. The plans incorporate several revolutionary new concepts which, for obvious reasons, must be kept top secret. We're meeting in Athens——'

'Excuse me,' Polly broke in, 'but who is this *we* you keep talking about?'

'A group of businessmen who, like me, want to see a British team regain the trophy. It costs many hundreds of thousands to mount a challenge like this. And even though a win would turn the investment into millions, naturally I don't want to commit that amount of finance entirely by myself.'

'Oh, naturally,' Polly murmured, her mind boggling. Was it just entrepreneur's hype that had made him say 'don't want to' rather than 'can't'? Or was he genuinely that rich?

'What's so amusing?' he enquired.

She shook her head. 'The way you talk about money.'

He waved a dismissive hand. 'You'll get used to it.'

'Of course I will,' she agreed blithely. Was he mad? What opportunities was she likely to have to *get used* to talking in millions?

'Now, if I may finish answering your question?' His tone made it clear that further interruptions would be neither welcome nor wise.

Despite her spirited independence Polly was unwilling to push him too far. The power of his personality was awesome. He presented this bland smiling façade, yet one glance from those glacial blue eyes could dry her mouth and stop her breath in her throat. Taking refuge in dignified silence, she simply nodded.

'To enable discussions of the project to take place in total secrecy,' he said, 'I'm taking my four colleagues cruising in the Cyclades. The original plan was for *Seawitch* to be delivered to the marina by the tenth and we'd fly in to join her there.' His features hardened. 'It was my charter company who recommended Kemp to me.' His expression left Polly in no doubt that someone would pay for that mistake when he returned to England. 'Then Clive didn't *steal* your boat at all,' she realised.

'I never said he did,' Nathan returned coldly. 'That was *your* assumption. He obviously had his own reasons for wanting you to believe he owned *Seawitch*. Perhaps he was trying to impress you.'

Polly's eyes widened. 'Why on earth would he want to do that?'

Nathan's eyes narrowed slightly. 'Are you serious?'

She was bewildered. 'It made no difference to me whether the boat *belonged* to him. He was the skipper, I was the cook.'

His eyes glittering, Nathan shook his head. 'Why do I find such protestations hard to believe?'

Polly stiffened. 'Because you have a naturally suspicious and mistrusting nature?' she suggested acidly.

He eyed her for a moment. 'The point is,' he continued firmly, 'if Kemp is locked up he obviously isn't going to be available to do the job he was hired for. In fact, when he does eventually get out of gaol I intend to make sure he never again sets foot on any boat or property owned by my companies.' His eyes were as cold as polar ice, his mouth a brutal slash.

Though Polly had little sympathy for Clive after what he had put her through, this merciless dismissal of another man's entire future made her skin crawl.

Then Nathan smiled, unnerving her still further. No man had the right to be that handsome. Especially a man as hard and remorseless as Nathan Bryce.

Linking his hands, he leaned towards her slightly. His eyes had acquired a thoughtful gleam that made Polly's heart lurch erratically. She waited for him to continue speaking, but he simply studied her with a detached speculation that did nothing to soothe her ragged nerves. Unable to bear this silent examination a moment longer, she said the first thing that came into her head.

'Surely it wouldn't be difficult to find another skipper? Better still, why not simply fly to Athens from here and charter another boat from the Kalamaki marina?'

Impatience darkened his features. 'How do you think it would look to my consortium if the chief designer and managing director of Bryce International, one of the major manufacturers of ocean racers, turned up in any other yacht but his own?

'Besides,' something in his voice made her flinch, 'after this little episode I don't feel like entrusting *Seawitch* to anyone else. Nor do I have the time to go looking for a suitable crew.' He stood up, towering over her. 'Why should I, when you're already here?'

Polly leapt to her feet, appalled. 'You can't be serious.'

'I thought I'd made it clear.' He shrugged calmly. 'I don't joke about money.'

'You take far too much for granted,' she stormed. 'I wouldn't go with you if you were the last man on earth.' She lifted her chin, radiating defiance.

A man as handsome, as powerful, and as used to getting his own way as this one was a dangerous man to know. She must get away from Nathan Bryce as fast as she could.

His calm smile never wavered. 'You understand that bail is granted only under certain conditions?'

Polly's head started to spin. 'What? What conditions?' Apprehension strummed her taut nerves.

'You are being released into my custody,' Nathan's cool gaze held hers, 'which means you are required *by law* to remain with me until you appear at your trial. And the date for that has yet to be fixed.'

Before she had time to absorb all the implications of this statement he was speaking again.

'An enormous amount of time and money has already been poured into this challenge. The Athens meeting has taken months to set up. This last-minute change of dates is only the latest in a long line of difficulties we've had to overcome.' His mouth hardened to an implacable line. '*I* got the whole thing up and running. I don't intend to lose out now.'

He stood up, looking down at her with eyes like splintered ice. '*Seawitch* sails for Athens first thing in the morning. Either you sail with me or I withdraw bail.'

Polly leapt to her feet. 'You'd leave me *here*?' she choked as her gaze flew round the shabby, spartan room.

'This is an interview-room,' he reminded her. 'I doubt that a cell would be as comfortable.'

'Th-that's b-blackmail,' she spluttered.

'It's your choice,' he retorted flatly, and looked at his watch. 'You'd better make up your mind.'

Polly turned away from him, collapsing on to her chair once more. What was she to do? How could she tell him she had never done any ocean sailing before? Clive had said it didn't matter. They had plenty of time and, with the auto-helm, he could manage the boat alone. All she had to do was provide three good meals a day.

But everything was different now. With the meeting re-scheduled a week earlier a fast passage was vital. And that meant hard sailing, long hours, and working as a team. *With Nathan Bryce*? A man whose idea of democracy was everyone agreeing with what he had already decided?

Besides, how could she crew efficiently when she didn't have the faintest idea of what she was supposed to do?

The alternative, spending the time until her trial in gaol, made her feel queasy just thinking about it. It could be weeks. She would have to let her parents know, and her father would insist on paying her bail, which would certainly wreck their holiday plans. She couldn't do that. The debt was hers, and she had to pay it.

It couldn't be *that* difficult to sail a boat. She was strong, nimble, and a quick learner. She could handle that. But could she handle Nathan Bryce?

What was there to handle? He was a hard-nosed, tunnel-visioned businessman, concerned only with getting to his precious meeting on time. As far as he was concerned she was nothing more than a time-and-labour-saving device required for the voyage. When she considered the alternatives there was no choice.

Sucking in a shaky breath, aware she was taking the greatest gamble of her life, she returned to face him. 'You have yourself a crew, Mr Bryce.'

CHAPTER THREE

WHILE Nathan completed the paperwork with the police and Customs officers, Polly excused herself and found the toilet.

After rinsing her face and hands under the cold running water, she dried them on a couple of paper towels. A few swift strokes of the comb smoothed her bubbly curls into soft wings which lay neatly against her well-shaped head and feathered down the nape of her neck.

Her hands dropped to her sides as she gazed into the cracked mirror. The face staring back at her was wide-eyed and nervous. That wouldn't do at all. She had to project confidence. If she *looked* as though she knew what she was doing, she might just be able to bluff her way through.

One thing was certain—she wasn't staying in this building one instant longer than she had to.

Snatching up her bag and cardigan, she returned to the Enquiry office. Nathan glanced round and strode forward to meet her.

'Ready?'

'Need you ask?' Polly murmured, inclining her head with frosty politeness towards the men whose expressions reflected varying degrees of speculation. Colour surged to her cheeks. She dug her nails into her palm. What had he told them? She took a grip on herself. What did it matter? She had far more important things to think about, like how she was going to survive the next four weeks alone with a man whose quiet voice and manner hid a ruthlessness and determination that made steel look limp by comparison.

As they walked out on to the street Polly took in a lungful of crisp cool air, savouring her freedom. Then she shivered.

Immediately Nathan pulled her cardigan from over her arm and draped it around her shoulders. His hands lingered for a moment, his fingers hinting at a strength that made her throat tighten. She swallowed involuntarily.

'The season is still young,' he warned. 'Though the days are getting warmer, spring nights can be surprisingly cold.'

'So I'm beginning to realise,' Polly replied, clenching her teeth to stop them chattering. He was still without a sweater over his lemon T-shirt, but the drop in temperature didn't seem to be bothering him. It wouldn't dare, she thought wryly.

He looked down at her. 'I know what you want,' he said in that soft deep voice that made her think of a silk-sheathed scalpel.

She moistened lips suddenly and inexplicably dry. 'I think that's most unlikely, Mr Bryce.'

His dark brows rose, his eyes gleaming in the reflected light. Polly felt the fine hair on her arms stand up, and apprehension danced like static electricity over her skin as he bent his head, his breath warm against her ear. 'Come on, own up—you'd kill for a good meal, a hot bath, and a soft bed. Will you settle for two out of three?'

Which two? Polly wondered instantly, and clamped her lips together so the words didn't spill out.

He led her to a waiting taxi and, as he held the door for her, for a brief instant their eyes met.

She knew he was laughing at her. A man of sophisatiction and wide experience, he recognised her lack of both and was teasing her like a cat playing with a mouse.

Somehow containing her fury, she flashed him a smile that would have made a lesser man shrivel. 'How thoughtful.' She climbed in.

'Not at all,' he demurred. After telling the driver to take them to the marina, he climbed in beside her. 'We have a demanding trip ahead of us, Miss Levington, and I have a lot of money invested in you.'

The thought of the twenty-five thousand pounds he had pledged in the belief that he was getting a skilled crew left her too daunted to frame a suitably crushing reply. So she remained silent as the taxi carried them towards the restaurants and bars that nestled beneath blocks of luxury flats overlooking the marina.

She felt like a tightrope walker suffering an attack of vertigo, terrified she was going to topple.

The taxi pulled up and they got out. After paying off the driver Nathan steered her into a busy, softly lit restaurant, and she had to admit he had guessed correctly that a meal did indeed top her list of priorities.

The rich, mouthwatering aroma of freshly cooked food made her stomach gurgle in anticipation. The sounds of animated conversation and laughter, the pop of wine corks and the chink of cutlery all combined to lift her spirits. She was free and among people again, people who were enjoying themselves.

As the shirt-sleeved waiter preceded them across the crowded room, Polly was startled when people began calling out to Nathan. He nodded and smiled, but he kept moving. Polly's cheeks grew warm, then hot, as she became aware of frankly appraising stares from both men and women.

'Fame must be such a bore,' she quipped, determined to show him how unimpressed she was by the eyelash-fluttering of the women and the hearty handshakes of their escorts as they traded banter and insults with him.

'If you can't stand the heat. . .' he shrugged. 'It has its uses.'

'So I see,' she muttered, waiting while he gently removed from his neck the clinging arms of a laughing woman who had plastered herself to his front.

'Getting a table in a crowded restaurant, for example.' The dry look he threw her over his shoulder as they followed the waiter to a small table in the corner stung her cheeks with colour.

Nathan nodded his thanks as the waiter presented each of them with a leather-bound menu. 'Gibraltar is a popular stop-over for boats heading for races off Greece, Yugoslavia and Turkey. Being in the same business, it's inevitable that we bump into each other all over the world. Crews and sponsors tend to frequent the same restaurants, pubs and hotels. We're a bit like fish,' he said drily. 'We move from place to place in shoals.'

Polly glanced round. 'Are *all* these people involved in ocean-racing, then?'

'Most of them. Then there are the usual bunch of hangers-on.'

'Who are they?' His scathing tone had fanned her curiosity.

'You mean apart from glamorous young women offering the kind of recreation not mentioned in tour guides?' She recalled his cynical reaction to her reason for sailing with Clive and felt her colour rise.

'Yes, apart from them.' Her reply was crisp and she

held his gaze, letting him see her anger. How dared he imagine she had anything in common with those girls?

'People who call themselves financial advisers, yacht brokers, design consultants, even journalists. But whose real job is picking up information.'

Polly blinked, not quite sure if he was serious. 'You mean. . .*spies*?

Nathan nodded, and this time there wasn't a glimmer of laughter in his flinty gaze.

'What sort of information?' she whispered over her open menu, fascinated yet uneasy at this glimpse into a world she had thought existed only in books or TV movies.

Nathan shrugged. 'It could be anything from a new sail shape or keel design to gossip about a skipper's sexual preferences.'

Polly's involuntary blush infuriated her. 'I don't see how that——'

He sighed impatiently. 'Do I have to spell it out? Ocean racing is big business involving vast amounts of money. Once a rumour starts to spread it affects concentration, not to mention morale. And that gives opposing teams an edge.'

'But if it isn't true——'

He shrugged. 'So what?'

Polly was appalled. 'Whatever happened to *sport*?'

Nathan's mouth quirked in a mirthless, sardonic smile. 'What a naïve little thing you are. Shall we order?'

Remembering just in time that this heartless cynic was responsible for getting her out of the clutches of the Gibraltar Police and Customs Service, Polly managed to bite back the caustic retort trembling on the tip of her tongue and stared blankly at the vast selection of starters and main courses.

Nathan closed the folder and laid it on the starched tablecloth. 'Might I suggest Brie fritters, followed by baked fish, with shredded lettuce, lemon slices, and rice flavoured with fresh herbs?'

Polly looked up. The waiter had returned, and was hovering respectfully as he waited to take their order. She closed her own menu. This was not the moment to make a stand for independence. There would be plenty of time for that. Besides, he had chosen a tasty nourishing meal which would not lie too heavily on her achingly empty stomach. She nodded her agreement. 'That sounds delicious.'

But when he ordered a bottle of chilled white wine she said quickly, 'Not for me.'

His face hardening, Nathan nodded briefly at the waiter. When the man had gone he rested his folded arms on the table. Polly was acutely aware of the contrast between his bronzed skin and the spotless white linen.

'Miss Levington,' his soft drawl had a brutal edge, 'as this is a business trip, not a pleasure cruise, I intend to spend my nights *sleeping*. I find a glass or two of wine aids the digestion and makes an excellent nightcap. However, it's not compulsory.' His smile was pleasant, but his gaze held contempt. 'I hope I make myself clear?'

Furious that she had no control over the scarlet tide that flooded her face at his insinuation, Polly clasped her hands tightly under the table. If he had written it in letters of fire he couldn't have made it plainer. He was not trying to get her tight. He didn't find her remotely attractive, and the meal and wine were simply fuel to replenish spent energy, not a prelude to seduction.

'*I* understand perfectly, Mr Bryce.' Polly's smile was

glacial. 'However, your vanity has made a fool of you. I don't drink because alcohol gives me a headache. I sleep like a log and never get indigestion. Other people's methods of handling those problems, or any others they may have, for that matter, are of no interest to me whatever. I hope I make *myself* clear?'

His surprise was fleeting but unmistakable. But Polly's pleasure at having scored a valuable point was tempered by fury. Who the hell did he think he was? How dared he assume her refusal of wine was in any way connected with him? He was, without doubt, the most arrogant, self-opinionated man it had ever been her misfortune to meet.

As he opened his mouth to reply he was interrupted by a polite cough. They both looked up to see a short, wiry little man who had been table-hopping beaming down at them. He had carefully groomed silver hair and skin like seamed leather. His lizard eyes, as they flicked from Nathan to Polly and back again, were alight with curiosity, yet there was no warmth in them.

'Nathan, my dear friend, how are you?' he gushed. 'I must admit I'm surprised to see you here.' He glanced at Polly again. 'Especially in the circumstances.'

Though he rose to his feet, Nathan did not shake hands with the newcomer. 'Hello, Louis.' He made no move to introduce Polly. 'And what circumstances are those?'

The little man made a production out of glancing round to see if anyone was listening. 'The problem you're having with the new keel, of course.' His smile was as smooth and glossy as patent leather.

After a split-second's hesitation Nathan sighed. 'Well, if *you've* heard I guess everyone knows.'

'I imagine so,' the little man nodded, his sympathy

transparently false. 'It's always the bad news which travels fastest. And for all of us there's so much at stake.'

Nathan sighed again. 'If we can't get it sorted I may have to pull out.'

The little man's face was avid, glee battling with commiseration. 'Surely not? After all your successes? That would be such a shame.'

Nathan spread his hands. 'You can't win 'em all.'

'No, no, indeed. It is, as the saying goes, an ill wind. Perhaps the time has come for another name to be engraved on the trophies. Your attitude does you credit. But then,' Louis flashed another glossy smile as he delivered the final stab, 'the British are such good losers. Enjoy your meal.' He was already moving away. 'So glad to have seen you.'

'I bet you are,' Nathan muttered drily as he sat down again.

'I'm sorry,' Polly said quietly. 'I had no idea. What rotten luck. It must be an awful strain.'

He looked mildly startled. 'I beg your pardon?'

She leaned closer. 'This business about the keel,' she whispered.

Their heads were only inches apart. Nathan's eyes were unreadable as they looked deep into hers. Then, before she could move or speak, his hand cupped her head and he pulled her forward, covering her mouth with his in a swift bruising kiss.

Frozen with shock, she stared at him as he leaned back in his chair. Her whole body was aflame, with rage, embarrassment, and beneath them something else, an elemental thrill that terrified her. It wasn't so much *what* he had done, though it was the very last thing she had expected, it was the way it had felt, like a high-voltage jolt of electricity. It left her dry-mouthed with excitement, yet she didn't even *like* him.

Nathan smiled at her. 'There isn't any problem with the keel.'

She stared at him, stunned. '*What*?'

'But I was touched by your sympathy.'

The arrival of the waiter with their fritters jerked her back to full awareness of her surroundings. Glancing surreptitiously around, she glimpsed knowing smiles and heads drawn close as people whispered.

Polly bent her head, masking her burning face with a trembling hand as she smoothed the feathery curls on the nape of her neck.

Nathan shook out his napkin. 'Louis probably started that rumour himself.'

She rubbed her temples. 'I don't understand. Why would he do that?' And why had Nathan Bryce kissed her? He had made a public spectacle of them both. There were times and places for behaviour like that, and this was neither. Even if they were fond of each other, which they most definitely weren't. So why had he done it?

'Louis is a financial freebooter,' Nathan said quietly. 'A wheeler-dealer with fingers in a number of pies, some of them very shady. His syndicate is new to ocean racing. He's trying to buy respectability. No doubt it's also a tax dodge. But that's not enough for Louis. The boat bearing his name and company logo has to *win*, and he'll use every trick in the book to boost his chances.'

The waiter reappeared with the bottle of wine Nathan had ordered. Polly poured herself some water from the carafe on the table.

Nathan tasted the wine and, as the waiter left after

filling his glass, he raised it. 'I won't ask if I can tempt you.'

Despite his deadpan expression, Polly sensed he was not referring solely to the wine.

A pang of yearning stabbed her, but she banished it at once. Was she mad? The wounds Giles had inflicted were only just beginning to heal. Had she ever really meant anything to him? Or had all his compliments and charm, so convincing at the time, been just a charade to get him what he wanted? *'If you really loved me you would. . .'*

Had she learned nothing? Did she want to be just one more notch on Nathan Bryce's bedpost? Because that was all she ever would be to a man like him.

'Very wise,' she agreed tartly. 'A refusal often offends. Male egos are so fragile.'

He lifted his glass higher in a silent mocking salute.

Despite a flaring anger at this impertinence her eyes were drawn to the strong column of his throat as he swallowed. Then she realised he was watching her, his heavy-lidded eyes gleaming with amusement and speculation.

Feeling the blush mount in her cheeks, she looked down quickly and, picking up her knife and fork, forced herself to start eating.

After the first melting mouthful reminded her how hungry she was, it was much easier to push disturbing visions and hurt-filled memories to one side and devote her attention to the food.

'Aren't you going to ask why?' Nathan drawled.

Polly's head came up sharply. But she was learning fast. 'Perhaps you'd better tell me what you're referring to,' she replied warily.

'Not introducing you to Louis.'

Thank goodness she hadn't mentioned the kiss. No

doubt he had already forgotten all about it. After all, it hadn't meant anything. In fact, it was so totally unimportant that she really had no idea why it hadn't slipped her mind as well.

She lifted one shoulder in a semi-shrug. 'You didn't introduce me to anyone else either. So assuming it wasn't bad manners or simply an oversight, you must have had a reason.'

He nodded. 'I did, but you won't like it.'

'There are quite a few things about today I haven't liked, Mr Bryce. One more won't make much difference.'

'Nathan, please.' As she opened her mouth to protest he added, 'Humour me.' And despite his smile and the teasing note in his voice, the look in his eyes said it was an order.

Realising she had no chance of winning an argument against the use of first names when they were about to spend several weeks alone at sea together, Polly made a brief gesture of acquiescence.

'And what do I call you?' he enquiried.

'Madam?' she suggested.

His eyes narrowed dangerously and for a split-second Polly held her breath. But then she noticed that the corners of his mouth were twitching and realised he was finding it hard not to laugh. 'You certainly are different from most of the young women I meet, Miss Levington,' he observed thoughtfully.

'You mean I have a *brain*,' Polly flashed him her sweetest smile. Then, giving him no chance to respond, she said, 'I was christened Paula Mary Josephine, but everyone calls me Polly.' She placed her knife and fork side by side on her empty plate. 'All right, why didn't you introduce me?'

'Because it suits me for Louis to believe I have

problems, and that I'm trying to forget them in the arms of an attractive young woman I'm not willing to share.' He took another drink, watching her all the time.

Polly swallowed, her mouth suddenly dry at the thought of those bronzed and powerful arms holding her close against his lean, hard-muscled body as, with a warning glare, he kept those who would come between them at bay.

It wasn't easy to maintain a light level tone as she asked, 'Is that the way you usually deal with problems? By running away from them?' The images his words had triggered were running riot in her brain, and it took all her strength to blot them out.

'No,' said Nathan, refilling his glass.

'Then why let that awful little man think it is?'

'You tell me.'

Having expected him to justify his actions, Polly was taken aback by his response.

'Come on,' he insisted. 'You're so proud of this brain of yours. Let's see it in action.'

Furious with him, and with herself for walking into the trap, Polly re-ran the conversation between the two men. Her frown clearing, she looked up. 'If *you've* got problems with your boat then *he* has one less competitor to worry about.'

'Exactly. And with Louis concentrating on the other competitors, there's a good chance my meeting in Athens will go completely unnoticed.'

'But what about *your* team's morale and concentration?' Polly asked.

Nathan smiled. 'My team are winners. They know better than to believe anything they hear, unless I'm the person who tells them.'

'What about me?' she demanded.

His eyes glittered. 'Do you really think I'm the kind of man who would run from *anything*?'

'That's not what I meant,' Polly cried. 'I agreed to sail with you as cook. . .and crew,' she forced herself to add. 'Having it spread around the Mediterranean that I'm another of Nathan Bryce's bimbos was not part of the deal. And you're right, I don't like it.'

'But that's precisely why I *didn't* introduce you to Louis,' Nathan reminded her smoothly. 'Neither he nor anyone else knows who you are.'

'That's not the point!' Seething with anger and frustration, Polly pushed back her chair and stood up. Immediately, he rose to his feet. It appeared to be no more than a gesture of politeness, but Polly knew he was poised to block her slightest move towards the door.

Not that she intended trying to leave—she had nowhere to go. Besides, jumping bail would make her a criminal. That was something she couldn't face. Being accused and knowing she was innocent had been bad enough.

Yet the longer she spent with Nathan Bryce the harder it was to accept that for the next four weeks her only escape from him would be in sleep. *But what if she dreamed. . .?*

'Excuse me,' she said with exaggerated politeness, 'I'd like to freshen up.'

Nathan's brows rose. 'This seems an odd time to choose.'

'That's women for you,' Polly retorted blithely.

'You wouldn't think of trying to leave without me, would you, Polly?' His soft words had a steely undertone of warning that was reflected in his eyes.

'Why don't you bribe a waiter to stand outside the door?' she snapped back, then stalked past him without a backward glance, acutely aware of the small smile playing at the corners of his mouth as his gaze followed her. *Blasted man.*

She came out of the cubicle to find a woman in a figure-hugging red dress, with a plunging neckline that revealed most of her tanned bosom, repairing her lipstick in the mirror above one of the washbasins. As Polly rinsed and dried her hands she was aware of being studied.

The woman closed her purse with a snap. 'How did you do it?' she demanded, her tone a mixture of curiosity and envy.

Polly's head flew round. 'Pardon me?'

'Oh, that's good. That's very good.' Malice sharpened the woman's features, and Polly realised that beneath the artfully applied make-up she was nearer forty than thirty. 'Playing the wide-eyed innocent, are we?' She smoothed the clinging dress over her hips, eyeing herself in the glass. 'It might just work, for a while. Men are so easily deceived.'

Shaken, but determined not to show it, sensing that any sign of vulnerability would lay her open to further attack, Polly drew herself up. 'I haven't the faintest idea what you're talking about,' she said icily. Lifting her bag from the shelf, she slung the strap over her shoulder and turned to go, only to find that the woman had placed herself between her and the door.

'I'm talking about Nathan Bryce.' The woman glanced at her reflection, fluffing her expensively streaked hair, then smoothing one finely plucked eyebrow with a fingertip.

To Polly the long, crimson-enamelled nails looked as though they had been dipped in blood. And the hostility she saw in the woman's eyes made her shudder inwardly.

'How on earth did you hook him? I've never known

him go for the skinny boyish type before.' She sighed indulgently, but her eyes were cold and furious. 'Men are so fickle, so easily bored, always on the look-out for something new and different.' Her glance raked Polly from head to toe. 'But you won't last a week,' her tone was scathing. 'Nathan needs a woman, not a simpering virgin.'

Polly swallowed. Was it that obvious? Her heart thumping against her ribs, she tilted her chin, fighting a confusion of emotions, some of which she didn't dare examine too closely.

'I have not *hooked* Nathan Bryce,' she snapped, her cheeks on fire as a kaleidoscope of images whirled through her brain. 'Nor do I want to.'

She determinedly ignored the vivid memory of his kiss, so brief yet as indelible as a brand.

She was grateful, that was all. If he hadn't posted bail for her she would now be preparing for her first night in jail. But gratitude was *all* she felt, and even that was overshadowed by anger at the way he had blackmailed her into sailing with him.

'What we have is purely a business arrangement.' Too late Polly realised that her words were open to a very different interpretation from the one she intended, and her heart sank as the woman's face creased into a hard-edged cynical smile.

'Oh, he's *paying* you, is he? Well, I suppose you do have some novelty value. What's the going rate these days?'

Reeling under the dreadful insult, Polly tilted her chin a little higher, determined not to let the woman see her hurt and fury. 'I'm sure you know more about such things than I do,' she replied, amazed that she could sound so calm.

She watched the barb strike home, then delivered

her parting shot. 'But Nathan Bryce has just parted with twenty-five thousand pounds in order to have me with him.'

As the woman's mouth sagged open Polly walked past her to the door.

'That's ridiculous,' the woman spluttered. 'You're lying.'

Polly shrugged lightly. 'Ask him,' she retorted, and marched out, leaving the woman staring speechlessly after her.

But as she made her way back to the table, Polly's fierce satisfaction at having the last word in what had been a nerve-shattering encounter quickly faded.

First Nathan had thought she was easy because he had seen her with Giles. His opinion had been reinforced by the fact that she had agreed to sail with Clive. Now this woman, a complete stranger, was saying the same thing because she was with Nathan. She felt angry and degraded.

'Everything all right?' Nathan enquired as she resumed her seat.

'Yes, thank you,' she replied curtly.

'You seem a little tense.'

'Tense? Me?' Polly's laugh was brief and bitter. 'What possible reason could I have for being tense? As if I hadn't been through enough today, I've just been dubbed your plaything of the week——'

'*What?*' The look on his face literally stopped her breath.

'You heard.' There was no way she was going to boost his ego by repeating the slander. 'But apart from that everything's fine, wonderful, couldn't be better.'

'That's good.' Nathan gave a bland smile. Not a trace remained of the cold rage that had set his face like granite.

Polly's fury doubled. How dared *he* be angry? It was *she* who had been insulted. Only the waiter arriving with their main course stopped her telling Nathan Bryce exactly what she thought of him and his female acquaintances. The effort of holding it all in made her feel as though she was about to explode.

'It does seem,' Nathan mused as the waiter departed once more, 'that things are working out quite well after all.'

'For you, maybe.' Polly attacked her fish.

'Now how can you complain?' There was something in his voice that made the hairs on the back of her neck stand up. 'After all, even though Clive Kemp is locked up, you're still making the trip you'd looked forward to so much.'

The succulent fish turned to sawdust in Polly's mouth and she had difficulty swallowing. Holding the glass tightly so that her hand wouldn't shake, she sipped the cool water, then met his gaze. 'Let's not pretend I had a choice. The conditions amounted to blackmail.'

'No, no, no,' he contradicted gently. 'It was a business agreement.'

Food forgotten, Polly glared at him. 'Is that how you measure everything in life?' she demanded, struggling to control her voice. 'By whether or not it's good *business*?'

His calm smile never faltered. 'Given that I'm a businessman, what else would you suggest?'

'And I suppose it's just too bad if people get hurt,' she cried. 'The end justifies the means. Secure the deal and to hell with integrity or compassion.'

His features hardened. 'Who's been hurt? I've just got you released from jail. Given that you, not I, were arrested, whose integrity is open to question? And as for compassion, haven't I just provided your first decent meal of the day? But of course,' his tone flayed like a whip, 'you've never done a dishonest thing in your life.'

As she opened her mouth Polly remembered she had deliberately withheld the fact that she couldn't sail. She swallowed quickly and moistened her lips. 'It isn't my morals that are being questioned.'

'No?' he said softly. 'Then what else has today been all about?'

Polly glared at him. Then she felt the blood drain from her face as she realised he was right. The Customs men had believed she was a drug-smuggler; Nathan had assumed she had virtually jumped out of Giles's bed and into Clive's. And that dreadful woman in the ladies' cloakroom—no, *that* didn't bear thinking about.

For though the thought of making love with either Giles or Clive made her cringe in distaste, imagining Nathan Bryce's arms around her, his mouth plundering hers as he moulded her against his powerful, hard-muscled length, sent hot sweet sensation lancing through her body.

Shocked, and bitterly ashamed at the treachery of her own feelings, Polly bent her head to hide her flushed face. How could she even *think* such things about a man whose reputation as a womaniser rivalled Casanova's? Where was her pride? Her self-respect?

Giles's taunts about her sexual naïveté had stung. Though he had gone through the motions of caring she saw now with the painful wisdom of hindsight that, despite all his assurances of love and respect for her, he had really only been interested in his own pleasure, pursuing it with all the subtlety of a bulldozer.

With Clive the situation had never arisen. If it had, she would have handled it with a decisiveness that left no room for misunderstandings.

But Nathan Bryce had only to look at her for her heart to skip a beat, then race out of control. Just being near him made her skin exquisitely sensitive. His briefest touch was an electric shock. All her senses were highly tuned to him.

It didn't mean anything, she told herself fiercely. She'd had an extremely stressful day. Things had got a bit out of proportion. A good night's sleep would see her back to normal—sensible and rational, and perfectly capable of ignoring such ridiculous flights of fancy.

Polly set down her knife and fork, unable to face another mouthful. Suddenly she was aware of her cardigan being draped around her shoulders and slowly she looked up to see Nathan standing beside her. Taking her arm, he drew her to her feet, his body shielding her from the rest of the room.

She stood quivering in his grasp, terrified he might somehow guess what she had been thinking. His warm hand sliding down to clasp hers was both comfort and torture.

'There's nothing wrong. I'm fine, really,' she blurted, stretching her mouth into a smile which she sensed didn't quite come off.

Nathan's face was unreadable. 'I think it's time we went back to the boat.'

CHAPTER FOUR

THEY made their way along the marina without speaking. But it wasn't a comfortable, companionable silence, at least not for Polly. She felt emotionally battered and thoroughly outraged. None of this mess was of *her* making, yet she was just as much a prisoner as if she had been in gaol like Clive.

Her spirit had been severely dented by the shocks of the past twelve hours. But, regardless of how she felt, she *had* to put on a good face. Her pride and self-respect demanded it.

Straightening her spine, she shot him a glance. 'I suppose it's too much to expect that you might look at what's happened today from *my* point of view.'

'Why should you think that?'

Polly found his tone of polite enquiry and total absence of facial expression disconcerting. She hadn't a clue as to what was going on in his mind. No doubt this ability to mask his thoughts and feelings was vital in the cut-throat world he inhabited, but she found it unnerving. It was like being lost in the dark. You couldn't see the signposts.

'Because men are only really interested in two things—money and status.'

Nathan looked down at her, one heavy brow rising. That was something else she found maddening, the fact that he towered over her. Not that she felt threatened, at least, not physically. But it did give him yet one more advantage in a situation already loaded against her.

At five feet eight she was above the average height for a woman. And when she wore heels she was frequently taller than the men she worked for—a situation which, to her amusement and relief, they seemed to find slightly intimidating.

Unfortunately, this had not held true with her last boss. His inability to keep his hands to himself had led to her resignation. The unexpected break, hard on the heels of her disaster with Giles, had nudged her into accepting Clive's invitation. Which in turn was responsible for the disastrous mess she was in now. Damn all men, Polly thought fiercely.

'This idea about men caring only for money and status,' Nathan said thoughtfully, 'is it a long-held opinion, or one you've arrived at recently?'

There was no trace of a smile on his face, so why did she have the feeling he was laughing at her? 'Today has merely confirmed years of observation,' she retorted stiffly.

'Cynicism doesn't become you,' he chided, his eyes ocean-deep as they reflected the lights at the edge of the marina. 'You're far too young and beautiful to——'

'Don't patronise me,' Polly flared, furious at the treacherous thrill his words provoked. He probably had a Master's degree in flattery. 'I'm twenty-four. Hardly a child.'

'But not yet a woman,' he said softly.

Grateful that the darkness hid her fiery blush, Polly clutched her cardigan more closely around her. She might as well be wearing a notice. How could she possibly tell him that her limited sexual experience was a matter of choice, not lack of opportunity? She could just imagine him saying, 'Yes, of course,' while his eyes betrayed amusement and pity.

The temporary nature of her job, staying only a few weeks at any one place, meant she had met and worked for a wide variety of men. Though pleasant and friendly, she had always kept her professional and private lives totally separate, making it quite clear that, for her, business and pleasure did not mix.

What strange quirk of fate had forced her into working for Nathan Bryce—the most handsome, fascinating and ruthless man she had ever met? She had always been a confident, outgoing person. So how was it he could make her feel uncertain and inadequate, yet set her a-quiver with treacherous delight at his lightest touch?

'My private life is none of your business,' she said tightly.

'It is when you expect me to accept a pronouncement about men offered as fact and founded on ignorance,' he responded at once. 'However, you do have a point.'

Polly's eyes widened. He was *agreeing* with her?

'Man is by nature a hunter,' he went on before she had a chance to speak. 'But civilisation has changed the ways in which he can express this instinct. Instead of facing some fierce wild animal alone and killing it armed only with courage and a spear, he now channels his competitive instinct into his job, or sport.' One corner of his mouth lifted in a self-mocking grin. 'It can still be pretty hazardous, though not quite so bloody.'

Polly didn't answer. She couldn't. Her mind was locked into a vision of Nathan, his bronzed body gleaming with oil and sweat as he ran in silent relentless pursuit of his terrified prey. Only it wasn't a wild animal he was hunting, it was her. She could hear her own heartbeat, feel her own mouth-drying fear.

They had reached the boat. He stepped on to the deck, then down into the cockpit and, turning, held out his hand.

'I can manage,' she said firmly, shaking her head in an effort to banish images which frightened her, but enthralled her as well. Such thoughts were dangerous. She climbed down after him, her gaze drawn to the way his back tapered beneath the stretchy material of his T-shirt from heavily muscled shoulders to the narrow waist and lean hips of a man in peak physical condition.

He unlocked the companionway hatch that led to the yacht's interior, glancing over his shoulder as he folded the doors back. 'I'm sure you've noticed how some older men believe their image is enhanced by being seen in public with beautiful young women.'

'Oh, yes,' Polly said drily, 'I've noticed.'

He glanced up at her from the bottom of the ladder. 'How do you feel about that?'

'It's none of my business,' she replied, gripping the solid wood grab-rails as she went down the five steps with their non-slip treads.

'It seems to make you a little uncomfortable,' he observed. 'Why?'

Turning to face him, Polly shrugged. 'I don't know. It's just. . .' After a moment's hesitation she blurted, 'The couples I've seen seem to *parade*, as though they want everyone to notice them.'

'Perhaps they're proud of each other,' Nathan suggested.

Polly shook her head decisively. 'No,' she frowned, searching for the right words. 'Their pride is not for each other, it's for themselves. As if they're saying, "look at me, see what I've got".'

She felt hot and sticky, and there seemed to be far

less room at the bottom of the companionway than she remembered. Nathan had engineered this conversation. He was leading up to something, but she had no idea what.

'Then if these beautiful young women are not in love with their elderly escorts,' Nathan's voice was soft and mildly puzzled, 'what do you suppose is the attraction?'

'It's obvious,' Polly retorted. 'The man is probably wealthy and important.' The moment the words left her lips she saw the trap, but it was too late. She was neatly caught.

'Ah,' he murmured with a cold ironic smile. 'Money and status. Perhaps that's all women are really interested in.'

'No, it's not,' Polly cried. 'How can you say that?'

'Personal experience?'

Beneath his dry tone she heard an echo of her own pain. It startled her. Had he been hurt too? She mocked her own naïveté. It would be a cold day in hell before Nathan Bryce allowed any woman within touching distance of his emotions.

'Then you should choose your. . .friends. . .more carefully,' she responded, oddly breathless, her heart thudding unevenly.

He gave an ironic snort of laughter. 'Like you did?'

'I haven't had your practice,' Polly retorted, colouring.

He shook his head, exasperated and cynical. 'You make it sound so easy.'

'What's so difficult?' Polly demanded.

'You don't have the faintest idea what sort of life I lead, do you?'

'You're joking,' she sniffed. 'Most of the people in Britain know the basic facts about your life.' Affecting boredom, she ticked the points off on her fingers. 'You've made a fortune by combining your talent for yacht design with a keen business brain. You've won so many cups, shields and tankards, you've cornered the silver market. You travel all over the world and stay in the top hotels where every room has its own sauna, jacuzzi, and hot and cold running maids. And let's not forget the Nathan Bryce Adoration Society.'

'The *what*?' In the glow from the marina lights his eyes had the sheen of hard blue steel.

Apprehension dried Polly's throat and she could feel her cheeks burning, but she had gone too far to stop now. Nor did she want to. He was good at dishing it out. It was about time he learned how it felt to be on the receiving end for a change.

'Oh, come on, no false modesty, please,' she chided. 'You know perfectly well that there are scores of women who would do literally anything for a night out, or in, with you.'

'You're exaggerating.' He was dismissive.

'No, I'm not. I've *heard* them talking about you.' Polly recalled that evening in the ballroom.

His eyes blazed briefly, and he seemed about to say something. Instead his lips compressed, as if he were physically stemming a tide of words, and he slung his briefcase on to the bare chart table. 'Yup, I've got it made. Everything a man could ask for.' He turned away to open the case.

Polly didn't understand the bitterness at the corners of his mouth. She was acutely aware that the whole ambience of the boat had changed. But the tension in the atmosphere had nothing to do with the events which had taken place on board earlier that day.

'I think,' Nathan's voice had an odd rasp as he pulled out a wad of papers and dropped them on the table, 'you'd better get some sleep. We have an early start tomorrow.'

The boat moved restlessly beneath them, as if impatient to be out on the open sea.

Polly moistened her lips. If she didn't make a stand now he would expect her to jump to his bidding for the rest of the voyage. She would do her share, but as an equal, not a servant.

'I'd like a shower first,' she said. 'There won't be time in the morning.'

'As you wish.' He turned towards the short passage on the left of the companionway, at the end of which lay the skipper's cabin. 'I'm going to unpack, then I have some paperwork to do. Do you know how everything works?'

'Yes, thanks,' Polly said over her shoulder, mentally crossing her fingers as she headed in the opposite direction towards her own cabin in the bow. That morning she had only been on board a couple of hours before being hauled off by the Customs men.

Clive had given her a lightning tour of the boat as soon as they arrived, but then he'd disappeared up on deck to start the engine from the cockpit, leaving her to stow the shopping in the ice-box and cupboards and unpack her bag.

She had only just finished when he called her to join him and enjoy the view of Gibraltar from the sea. A short time later the Customs launch had borne down on them and the nightmare had begun.

After fiddling with the tiny shower-head Polly managed to get a spray rather than a trickle of lukewarm water. Remembering that all fresh water had to be stored on board, she turned it off while she soaped herself. It was wonderful to rinse off the lightly scented

lather and with it the heat and grime and terror of a
day she never wanted to repeat as long as she lived.

As she dried herself, banging her elbows against the
sides of the small compartment, she started to giggle.
How on earth did a man the size of Nathan Bryce
manage in here?

'Are you all right?' The sound of his voice made her
jump, despite the fact that he was on the far side of
the door.

'Wonderful!' she called back, fighting to control
laughter which was only a heartbeat from tears. Yet it
wasn't altogether a lie. She *did* feel better. The shower
had refreshed her. There was food in her stomach.
And in a few moments she would be in the privacy of
her own cabin, snuggling into a warm sleeping-bag on
a thick foam mattress with a fabric cover that matched
the padded headrest.

The fact that this comfort was all courtesy of Nathan
Bryce was something outside her control. Fate had put
her in the wrong place at the wrong time with the
wrong man.

After brushing her teeth Polly struggled into the
tracksuit she had brought along to double as a bath-
robe. She looked for her comb, but couldn't find it.
So, peering into the mirror fastened to the bulkhead,
she ran her fingers through her mop of damp curls,
then, tossing soap, flannel and toothbrush into the
zippered toilet-bag, she picked up her towel and
opened the door.

The shower-room and toilet, which Nathan called
the 'head', were alongside his cabin. There was also a
small washbasin set into a vanity unit with a cupboard
underneath for storing spare toilet rolls and various
cleaning materials.

Alongside *her* cabin was a hanging locker. She

wished with all her heart that the layout could have been the other way round.

As she turned the corner, about four feet ahead of her at the saloon end of the passage, Nathan was sitting in the well-padded swivel chair bolted to the deck in front of the chart table. Hunched forward, the lemon T-shirt tight across his broad shoulders, his thick hair curling untidily on his tanned neck, he was taking measurements from the chart and making notes on a pad.

'Goodnight, then,' she said, edging past.

Clive had told her the boat could sleep six quite comfortably when the settees on either side of the drop-leaf dining table were converted into sea-bunks.

Polly couldn't imagine it. For though the boat's interior was a masterpiece of functional yet elegant design which created an impression of light, airy spaciousness, the very presence of Nathan Bryce made it feel cramped and claustrophobic.

'Goodnight,' he muttered without looking up.

Polly didn't know whether to feel relieved or slighted. Then, smothering a yawn, she decided she was too tired to feel anything.

She went into her cabin. As she closed the door she glanced through the narrowing gap and saw Nathan toss down his pen, rest his elbows on the chart and rub his face.

The gesture betrayed more than simple fatigue. It revealed something she would never have associated with the man whose ironic half-smile appeared in tabloid gossip columns almost as often as it did in yachting magazines.

Polly leaned against the door. Nathan Bryce *lonely*? The stress of the day had given her delusions. He had people queuing up to spend time with him. He was

on every party guest-list. And if she opened the door
again any sign of the man she had just glimpsed, the
human being behind the impenetrable barrier, would
be instantly and totally erased. If he had ever existed
outside her overheated imagination.

Opening the glazed hatch above her head to allow
the cool night air into the small cabin, Polly threw off
her tracksuit, pulled on a clean thigh-length baggy T-
shirt, and slid into her sleeping-bag.

The mattress was shaped like a triangle to fit the
shape of the boat. Stretched out flat, her feet pointing
to the bow, she closed her eyes.

Seawitch moved gently on the water. Polly could
hear far-off voices and laughter, and the soft tapping
of metal halyards against masts. She turned over,
acutely aware of the man on the other side of the door
and angry at her own awareness. She moved restlessly,
searching for a cooler spot on the pillow, her mind
awhirl with fragmented images of Nathan Bryce as she
relived the swift bruising pressure of his lips on hers.
How would she ever sleep?

It seemed she had only just drifted off when she was
woken by a sharp rap on the door and Nathan's
impatient voice announcing, 'Breakfast in five
minutes!'

'Thanks,' she mumbled, still drugged with sleep.

The door opened and his head came round it. 'No,'
he corrected her brusquely, 'I *want* breakfast in five
minutes. You're here to work, so get moving. *Now*.'

Her eyes flying open, Polly reared up on one elbow.
She opened her mouth to fire a barbed reply, then,
remembering where she would have been waking up if
he hadn't bailed her out, she bit her tongue. Her
restraint was unnecessary. He had already gone.

She heard the companionway doors open and the

hatch slide back. Pulling on navy shorts and a pale blue polo shirt over her white lace bra and pants, she made sure the cabin skylight was open as far as it would go, then gave her sleeping-bag a brisk shake and spread it out on the mattress to air.

Grabbing her toilet-bag and towel, she rummaged in her bag for her comb. There was no sign of Nathan as she hurried through the saloon, but his cabin door was ajar and she couldn't resist peeping in as she passed.

Yesterday's jeans and shirt had been tossed on to the rumpled heap made by his sleeping-bag and two dented pillows. Feeling herself blush, but not sure why, she went quickly into the washroom and locked the door.

A new bar of soap, still wet and streaked with lather, lay in a dish on the lower shelf of the pigeon-hole storage area to one side of the basin. A battery-driven razor lay in another. A plastic tumbler containing toothbrush and paste stood on a deeper shelf behind two thin metal rails designed to prevent things falling off.

While part of Polly's brain noted the fresh fragrance of the soap and minty scent of toothpaste, the other part was registering for the first time the significance of plastic-covered grab-rails in the shower cubicle and on the front of the vanity unit. She swallowed. Surely it didn't get *that* rough?

Face washed, teeth cleaned, and her curly mop subdued by a damp comb, she placed her toilet things in another of the pigeonholes. It made sense to leave them where they would be used. It would also save time if she didn't have to carry them to and fro.

But though the logic was undeniable, she still felt a quivery sensation in her stomach as she placed her toothbrush in the tumbler next to Nathan Bryce's.

Dropping her folded towel on the curved edge of the kitchen worktop to remind herself to hang it out on deck later, she set about preparing breakfast.

She filled the kettle from the freshwater tap, then took a box of chilled orange juice from the well-stocked ice-box. Though the ice-box would continue to work at sea, run off the battery, the microwave could only be used while they were hooked up to the shore power supply. Polly popped three frozen bread rolls in, then made porridge and scrambled eggs on the two-ring gas burner, hunting for mugs and plates in the cupboards as she stirred.

Within minutes everything was ready. Setting it on the saloon table, and inhaling the delicious combination of smells, Polly went up the companionway ladder to call Nathan.

The sun had just risen and was beginning to burn away the mist. Entranced by the quiet calm, Polly stood in the cockpit gazing out over the stern. Hearing a sound behind her, she turned and saw Nathan approaching from the bow.

He was wearing a clean white T-shirt, frayed denim shorts, and navy canvas deck shoes, his dark hair already drying in unruly waves. As he came along the deck his legs were on a level with her eyes. Polly found herself staring at his thighs, mesmerised by the powerful muscles that bunched and flexed beneath bronzed skin dusted with gold-brown hair. Was he that colour all over?

As the thought sprang into her mind she felt her entire body flood with heat even as she shivered in the chilly air. 'A bit fresh, isn't it?' she said with a bright smile, rubbing her arms fiercely as she looked anywhere but at him. 'Though it's certainly a beautiful morning.'

'Is breakfast ready yet?' he demanded, ignoring her greeting. 'I want to get under way as soon as possible.'

'Yes, it's ready,' she replied crisply. 'That's why I came up, to tell you. Though even galley slaves need an occasional lungful of fresh air.'

'Then open the vents and hatches,' he suggested, automatically ducking to go down the companionway. 'There's nothing in our agreement which says you have to suffocate.'

Polly made a face at his back, then followed him. But, not yet used to leaping up and down the ladder, she was slower and more careful.

By the time she reached the bottom he had the saloon deck hatch open and was sitting at the table. Next to his plate was a jotting pad and pen which he must have picked up as he passed the navigation station.

'Shall I open yours?' she asked with a clenched-teeth smile.

Swallowing the last of his orange juice, he replaced the glass on the table. 'My what?' He looked up from the list he was making.

'Cabin hatch.'

He shook his head. 'It's already open. But you can make the bed.'

'Gosh, thanks,' she muttered, seizing her glass of orange juice. How many weeks of this could she take? 'You certainly intend making the most of this— situation.'

'Twenty-five thousand is quite a lot of money,' he pointed out. 'I think I'm entitled to something in return, don't you?'

Unable to argue with the fairness of his statement, Polly felt her anger and frustration double. What exactly *would* he expect from her? Quickly thrusting the thought away, she clattered the glass against her teeth, gulped a larger mouthful than she intended, and struggled desperately not to cough.

Nathan returned his attention to his notes and began to eat, wolfing down the food. Setting her glass aside, Polly followed suit. His obvious hunger made her wonder how long he had been up and about.

As he pushed away the empty plates she waited for him to make some comment about the meal. When he didn't she told herself she hadn't really expected any and actually preferred it this way. The more he had to think about, the less likely he was to bother her. But she wasn't used to being treated as though she didn't exist, and nor, despite her quip on deck, did she intend being a slave.

'More coffee?' she enquired sweetly.

Without even looking up from his notes Nathan pushed his mug towards her.

Polly poured the coffee, adding milk and three spoonfuls of sugar. She placed it within reach of his hand, then got up and began clearing the table.

She had her back to him when she heard him pick up the mug. She waited.

'Ugghhh!' he grunted, and the mug thumped down on the varnished wood.

Busy in the sink, Polly hid a mischievous smile.

'I don't take sugar.'

She looked over her shoulder, a picture of innocence and apology. 'Don't you? Oh, dear.'

He leaned back against the padded settee. There was no preoccupation now in the heavy-lidded gaze that slid lazily from her rapidly warming cheeks down her slim high-breasted body to her bare legs. Why hadn't she worn trousers or a skirt?

'Well?' One dark brow rose in sardonic enquiry.

Polly swallowed. She wanted to look away, but she couldn't.

'You have my undivided attention.' He paused. 'That *is* what you wanted, isn't it?' He seemed totally relaxed, but Polly was suddenly as nervous as a kitten.

'Nothing to say?' he goaded.

She bit her lip. No matter what she said it would sound defensive. It wasn't *fair*.

Rising to his feet, he picked up the mug and came towards her. She bent her head and scrubbed furiously at the plates.

The galley was shaped like a three-sided square, and by parking himself at right angles to the double sink, his back to the companionway ladder, Nathan had her trapped. The cooker was on her right and the worktop behind her.

He was so close that Polly could feel his body warmth and smell the soap he had used that morning. She couldn't even edge away. There was simply no room—the grab-rails in front of the sink and cooker made sure of that.

'In that case,' he said softly, 'there's something *I'd* like to say.'

'Oh?' She glanced up at him, and looked quickly back at the dishes as various possibilities chased through her mind.

'Yes. I want your word that you'll treat anything you see or hear while on board this boat as absolutely confidential.'

She glared up at him. 'You really are incredible. You won't accept that I knew nothing about the drugs, yet you want my word? If you knew anything about me, *Mr Bryce*,' she bristled, 'you'd realise your request is both unnecessary and offensive. Not only have I never handled any drug stronger than an aspirin, but discretion and confidentiality are an integral part of my job. The day after I finished working for the managing director of a certain company fighting off a take-over bid, the agency sent me to the rival company.'

Nathan studied her. 'And?'

'And nothing. That's the point. I've *always* treated everything I've seen or heard as absolutely confidential. As far as I'm concerned the person paying my salary has a right to expect total loyalty.'

'I'm not paying your salary.'

'You got me out of gaol. I'm working on your boat. The principle's the same.'

'And when you were on board with Clive Kemp,' he shot back, 'did *he* have your total loyalty?'

Knowing he was referring to the drugs, Polly recoiled as though he had struck her. 'No,' she whispered, then repeated the word with all the force she could muster. '*No!*'

He frowned. 'Do you realise you probably have information which, if offered to the right people, could make you one hell of a lot of money?'

'Of course I realise,' Polly snapped. 'I'm not stupid. But I'd be dropped faster than a hot brick if I betrayed a confidence. Money isn't everything, Mr Bryce. I enjoy working for the agency. And at least I can sleep at night.'

'Come from a wealthy family, do you?' There was an edge of cynicism to his enquiry.

The question took Polly aback. 'Well. . .' She hesitated, remembering the large rambling house she'd grown up in and the hours she had spent with Mrs Richards, their cook and housekeeper, who lived in a self-contained flat over the double garage.

Polly's parents had entertained a lot, and dinner for

up to twenty people two or three times a week was not unusual. They had had other help in the house too; Mrs Eddy from the village who came for three hours every morning, and her daughter Jess who waited at table for dinner parties and helped with the clearing up after. Then there was Tom the gardener.

'We certainly weren't poor,' she admitted. 'Though my sisters and I were never *given* pocket money. We had to earn it. We each had a list of chores, and if we didn't do them we didn't get paid. I learned the value of money very young.' She raised her head and looked him in the eye. 'But there are more important things in life, Mr——'

'Don't,' he warned softly. As he leaned towards her she instinctively recoiled, colouring furiously as he smiled. 'My name is Nathan.'

Damn him. He'd put it in such a way that she couldn't argue. He was stating a fact, not inviting intimacy. Half a dozen cutting remarks trembled on the tip of her tongue, but though she longed to hurl them at him, and watch him shrivel, she knew she couldn't. And what was even worse, *he* knew it too.

'Anyway, what has my family got to do with it?' she challenged.

'Nothing,' he shrugged lightly, pushing his hands into the pockets of his shorts. 'Except that it's easy to be indifferent to money when you've never been short of it.'

'And you have?' Sarcasm and disbelief coloured her voice, but she didn't care.

He gave a brief nod. 'Yes.' He turned, started up the ladder then paused. 'My father was one of the kindest men you could hope to meet. Unfortunately he was too trusting. Or, to put it another way, he had no head for business. People he looked on as friends took advantage of him.' He looked into her eyes. 'That appears to be one experience you and I have in common. Anyway,' his gaze shifted slightly and his tone grew harder, as if he regretted the revelation, 'he was forced out of business and lost the boatyard which had been in his family for four generations.'

'What happened?' Polly tentatively broke the lengthening silence.

Nathan's features were cold as he met her eyes once more, and she tensed, expecting a rebuff. But it didn't come.

'My parents wouldn't let me leave school, so I got a daily paper-round and weekend work at the local timber yard. To help pay off the debts my mother got herself a job. But physically she wasn't strong. She'd lost two babies before they had me. The demands of running a home, looking after my father and me, and going out to work, were too great. She died when I was fifteen.' His voice was totally devoid of emotion. 'Father blamed himself and just gave up. He lived another five years.' Nathan's face was bleak. 'If it could be called living. In the end he was glad to go. He never came to terms with losing her, or the fact that people he'd trusted cheated him.'

Polly swallowed hard. 'I'm so sorry.'

His dismissive gesture made it clear he didn't want sympathy. 'It taught me a lot about life, about being self-sufficient, and,' his voice hardened, 'about people.'

'I can understand you being bitter.' She was angry with herself for being moved by this completely unexpected glimpse into his past. She didn't want to feel warmth or compassion for Nathan Bryce. It would put her at even more of a disadvantage than she already was.

'I'm not bitter.' The way he said it forced her to believe him. 'I believe in the American motto: don't get mad, get even.'

'And have you?' she couldn't help asking.

His slow smile made her flesh creep. 'Oh, yes. The boatyard was to be my inheritance. I got it back. But in case you're wondering, no, I didn't.'

Polly gazed at him blankly. 'No, you didn't what?

'Make my fortune by cheating others. I'm a hard man, Polly. Some call me ruthless. But when *I* don't sleep, it's not my conscience that's keeping me awake.'

His gaze raked her body, returning to linger for a moment on her mouth. Then, without another word, he hauled himself up the ladder, leaving her wide-eyed, speechless, and so confused that she wanted to scream.

CHAPTER FIVE

POLLY finished drying the dishes and wiped down the cooker and the work surfaces, vaguely aware of the engine's deep rumble and the sensation of movement. She had concentrated hard on the mundane chores, hoping, unsuccessfully, to keep Nathan Bryce out of her thoughts.

The galley gleamed. She looked wistfully up the companionway to the square of blue sky, but fought the urge to go up on deck, scared he might ask her to do something that would reveal her ignorance. It would be wiser to stay out of sight a while longer.

In her own cabin she stowed her sleep shirt in a locker. She started to roll up her sleeping-bag, then hesitated. Far better to leave it opened out on the mattress to air. Plumping up the pillows, she set them against the padded headrest and left, closing the door behind her.

She felt like a cork tossed on the swirl and eddy of her own thoughts. Just when she thought she had Nathan Bryce weighed up he would reveal another totally unexpected side to his character. He had as many facets as a diamond, and was just as hard.

As she walked into his cabin, she could smell the faint elusive fragrance that was uniquely his, a blend of soap, shower gel, and the heady musk of clean warm male. She breathed him in, and the battle inside her intensified. She folded his discarded jeans and shirt and stowed them in a locker, then turned his sleeping-bag inside out and shook it. What had he done with

his pyjamas? The cabin simply wasn't big enough to
lose things in.

Then she realised, and felt heat flood her face. She
couldn't find them because he didn't wear any.

Her movements brisk and businesslike though her
mind was imitating a tumble-drier, she gave his sleeping-bag another quick but thorough shake and spread
it out over the mattress.

'Polly?'

She jumped as his voice reached her through the
open hatch. 'Yes?' Thank heaven he couldn't see her.

'Leave what you're doing and come up here.'

Oh, lord, what now? Reluctantly Polly joined him
on deck, aware that the engine had stopped.

'You bellowed, sir?' she enquired tartly, ignoring
the dread that coiled like snakes in her stomach. What
was he going to ask her to do?

He turned to study her, eyes narrowed, expression
thoughtful. 'Respect? From you?' he mocked. 'Now
why does that make me suspicious?'

Polly's heart gave a horrible lurch. He was far too
astute. 'Look, did you call me up here for a particular
reason? Only I have plenty to——'

'Take the wheel,' he cut in softly.

Startled, she gazed at him. 'Me?'

'I don't see anyone else around,' he replied.

She slid past him and curled her fingers around the
thin wheel with its padded sleeve. Nearly a metre
across and mounted on a sturdy pedestal which also
contained the compass, it looked oddly fragile, but
Polly knew that was deceptive. In fact, it was
immensely strong, yet light enough to be controlled
single-handed.

She had seen pictures taken on board ocean racers
which showed the helmsman steering though moun-

tainous seas with one hand while he operated the winch handle controlling the mainsail with the other. Her throat constricted. Was Nathan expecting *her* to do both?

Panic fluttered like dark wings inside her. 'Is—is there something wrong with the engine?' Her voice emerged a note or two higher than normal.

With a south-westerly wind filling her sails, *Seawitch* was slicing through the sparkling waves like a hot knife through butter.

Nathan looked surprised. 'No. I only ran it to get us clear of the bay and to charge the batteries.' He started to move away. 'Just keep her on her present heading.'

Polly glanced at the compass, tried desperately to imprint the numbers on a brain that seemed to have gone completely blank, then looked round at him. 'Where are you going?' Hearing the panic in her voice, she quickly added, 'I mean, will you want me up here for long? Only I'm——'

'Busy?' he supplied drily. 'Polly, *Seawitch* isn't a Cunard liner, and her design and fittings are all energy-efficient. It takes very little effort to keep her clean and tidy.'

'That depends on your standards,' she retorted.

He tilted his head to one side. 'Or could you have some reason for wanting to avoid me?'

He had completely ignored her remark, preferring his own theory.

Tossing her head, Polly clicked her tongue. 'Your vanity's showing again,' she warned. 'We're together through circumstances, not choice.' Though her tone was crisp, her insides were like jelly. 'You're simply not important enough for me to want to avoid you.' Silently praying she would be forgiven for the lie, she gave a small shrug. 'Sorry, but there it is.'

'You know,' he mused, gazing at her, 'for someone *apparently* so much in command of herself and the situation, you seem strangely nervous. Now why is that?'

Polly had to think quickly. They were still close enough to shore for him to return her to the police if she admitted she was not an experienced ocean sailor. Rather than have that happen she would take her chances on the boat.

But to deny being nervous when he *knew* that she was would be both pointless and stupid.

'Of course I'm nervous,' she retorted. 'Wouldn't you be, in my shoes? *Seawitch* is obviously very special to you, and I've never crewed for a world-famous yachtsman before.' That at least was totally honest.

Nathan's expression hovered between cynicism and puzzlement. 'Somehow I find it difficult to imagine you being overawed by anything.'

Polly gulped, and immediately disguised it with a cough. He had been studying her. The knowledge was petrifying. Yet at the same time his remark provoked a traitorous pang of delight.

The boat heeled in the freshening breeze. She braced herself and gazed at the compass, silently begging the needle to stop wavering to and fro.

'Hold her steady,' Nathan warned, and vaulted up on to the deck. 'Did you set the headsail yesterday?'

Polly didn't dare take her eyes off the compass. She moistened her lips. *She* hadn't set anything. She wouldn't even know where to start. But had Clive? 'I can't remember. We weren't on board very long. In any case——'

'You were down below, *busy*,' he finished with cutting mockery. 'I should have guessed. Nesting, are you?' The sneering curl to his lip made the question a deliberate insult.

Polly was both infuriated and unnerved. 'I beg your pardon?'

'Practising to be a good little wife?'

Livid, Polly sucked in a breath. 'Mr Bryce, wherever I'm living I like things clean and tidy. It has everything to do with personal standards, and absolutely nothing to do with a desire to get married. Only a *man*,' she invested the word with all the contempt she could muster, 'would assume otherwise.'

'Are you telling me you don't want to get married?' He was openly sceptical.

'I might, eventually,' she allowed. 'But right now I prefer freedom and independence.'

His mouth twisted in a derisive smile. 'Oh, you're one of the "love them and leave them" types. Get what you can and move on. I've known a few like you.'

The terrible injustice of his bitter words, echoing Giles's cruel slander, stabbed her to the heart. Had they been anywhere else but on the sleekly beautiful boat she would have rounded on Nathan with a devastating tirade and cut the ground from under his feet. But concentrating as she was on simply surviving, she had neither time nor energy enough.

'Why not?' she flung back at him. 'It's what *men* have been doing for centuries.' She drew in a shaky breath. The look on his face made her recoil inwardly. But though her cheeks flamed she held his gaze. 'Why are you asking about the headsail?' she enquired, steering the conversation on to less painful ground. 'Is something wrong?'

'One of the ropes seems to be jammed.' Though his tone was abrupt, Polly sensed a lessening of tension in him at the change of subject. She was overwhelmed by a mixture of terror and relief as he left her at the wheel and went forward to free the line. How long could she keep up the pretence of being a competent sailor?

She risked a glance back over her shoulder. The towering cliffs of Gibraltar were still all too clearly visible. She gritted her teeth. She *had* to keep going.

A few minutes later Nathan jumped down into the cockpit once more and hauled out the roller-reefed headsail. As it filled, *Seawitch* leaped forward. Nathan's gaze flicked over sails, lines, winches and compass, in a swift visual check.

Polly half turned, ready to return control of the boat to him.

'Right, I'll leave you to it, then.' He gave a brief nod, and swung himself down the companionway.

'Where are you going?' Even as the words left her lips she knew they sounded ridiculous. On a forty-foot yacht there weren't many places he *could* go. 'I—I mean, just in case. . .if I should need. . .anything.'

His hooded eyes were quizzical. 'I have several calls to make on the radio telephone.'

'Business as usual, even out here.' Polly shook her head in mock admiration, anxious to deflect his attention from herself.

'Of course it's business as usual.' He was curt. 'After all, this *is* my business. As for leaving you to sail the boat, what could possibly happen that you haven't handled before?'

As Polly turned her head away, terrified of betraying herself, he gave the knife several more twists by adding, 'Stop worrying. I trust you.'

She swung round. 'You do?'

His expression hardened. 'With my boat. No woman has ever skippered *Seawitch* before.'

Immediately Polly stepped backwards, offering him the wheel. 'If you'd rather not——'

He didn't let her finish. 'Forget it. You're here to share the workload. This is one of the perks. Relax, enjoy it while you can.'

Watching his dark head disappear, Polly conjured up some very satisfying visions of Nathan Bryce being chased by a shark with a mouth like a huge pair of pinking shears.

Then she was overcome by panic. Being the skipper meant she was in sole command of a million pounds' worth of yacht. She couldn't even control her trembling limbs and chattering teeth.

At that moment she would have willingly given her right arm to be anywhere but on Nathan Bryce's boat. She'd have given both arms to have avoided even meeting the blasted man. He was far too disturbing; an intimidating blend of magnet and menace.

She wanted to run away and hide. The responsibility was too great. Yet somehow one hand remained on the wheel and the other clasped the mainsail winch. As the seconds ticked by and *Seawitch* continued to cut a creamy path through the sapphire water, the tightness in her chest became a pain. She realised with a shock that, while waiting for the disaster she believed was inevitable, she had been holding her breath.

She let it out gently, not wanting to do anything sudden or jerky. Wincing at the stiffness in her fingers, she loosened her grip on the steering-wheel and was amazed at how much more responsive the boat felt. Or was it *she* who was more receptive?

Screwing up her courage, Polly altered course very slightly, turning the winch handle to let the mainsail out just a fraction. She watched the way the wind filled it and felt the boat dig deeper into the water, moving under her like some wild creature straining against a leash.

Her heart leapt with fright and she caught her lower lip between her teeth.

Forcing herself to keep her actions smooth and steady, she tightened the sail again and turned the wheel a few degrees the other way. *Seawitch* came upright, her movement more demure and restrained.

Polly grinned in delight, revelling in a heart-swelling sense of power. She had always loved to watch the sailing on Saturday afternoons and summer evenings when boats of every shape and size criss-crossed the wide estuary like multi-hued butterflies. Thrilled by the beauty of the scene, she had sometimes felt a twinge of envy for the people on board.

But now not only was she on board one of the arrow-like, tall-masted ocean racers she had so admired, *she* was actually in control.

'What are you doing?' Nathan's voice floated up from below.

Polly jumped. 'Just getting the feel of her,' she shouted back recklessly.

Not even the best vintage champagne could give this feeling of exhilaration. If the rest of the voyage was as smooth and simple as this, she didn't have a thing to worry about. At least, not as far as the *sailing* was concerned.

Totally absorbed in holding the course while at the same time tightening the mainsail as the breeze grew gusty and erratic, Polly was surprised when Nathan emerged from the companionway. 'Have you finished already?' she asked.

'Mmm.' He sat down. Resting his elbows on the deck behind him, he tipped his head back and closed his eyes. The white T-shirt pulled tight across his broad

chest. Caught by the breeze, the lower edge flipped
back to reveal a tautly muscled belly covered with fine
dark hair which arrowed down beneath the waistband
of his close-fitting denim shorts. Heaving a sigh, he
stretched his bronzed legs out. 'Enjoying yourself?' he
enquired.

Quickly dragging her gaze from his splendid body,
Polly stared with intense concentration up at the
mainsail, then down at the compass as embarrassment
flamed her face. How had he known?

Then common sense took over. He'd had his eyes
closed. He couldn't have observed her intent scrutiny
which was fuelled by an unfamiliar feeling she found
deeply shocking.

Raising heavy lids a fraction, he cocked a quizzical
eyebrow at her. 'Well? Are you?'

'Enjoying myself? I certainly am. This is fantastic.'
Her wide grin was partly relief. Let that be a lesson to
you, she warned herself sternly. Then, realising that for
a supposedly experienced sailor her enthusiasm was a
little over the top, she added quickly and with complete honesty, 'I've never sailed a boat like *Seawitch*
before. She's beautifully balanced and incredibly
responsive.'

'Boats and women,' he said in a voice that reminded
her of melting dark chocolate. 'It's all in the handling,
so I'm told.' Though his eyes were narrowed against
the sun, there was no mistaking the glitter in them,
and Polly felt her skin tingle as she coloured.

'So you're told?' she repeated drily. 'I had the
distinct impression you're an expert.'

'On boats,' he agreed.

'Not women?' She couldn't resist the ironic dig.
She'd put up with enough of them from him.

Turning his head, he gazed out over the stern, his

face as impassive as that of an Apache chief. 'Any man who claims to be an expert on women quite obviously isn't.'

It certainly wasn't the answer Polly had expected. 'You amaze me. Surely a man with your experience——'

'What would you know about my experience?' he cut in, his tone scathing.

'Well, obviously only what I read in the papers,' she began. 'But——'

'And you *believe* what you read in the papers?' His cynical taunt made her feel about fourteen.

'I tend to when the same story appears time and time again,' she retorted. 'Of course, the woman in the photographs with you is usually different. But the caption is always the same. "Nathan Bryce with his constant companion. . ."' she snorted. 'With so many constant companions to keep happy I'm amazed you find the time, not to mention the energy, to do any work at all.'

His mouth twisted. 'Every job has its drawbacks.'

'Mmm.' Polly gave a dry smile. 'It must be really tough being chased by hordes of gorgeous women.'

Irritation crossed his face. 'Most of them don't know the first thing about sailing.'

'And it's important that they should?'

'Of course.' He stretched. Deliberate or not, the movement made Polly acutely aware of his superb physique. She felt a wrenching tug of attraction and swiftly crushed it.

'After all,' he went on, turning the full force of his piercing gaze on her, 'you have to talk some time.'

Blushing, Polly glanced away. Yet she still saw his hard proud profile, softened only by the unexpected generosity of his mouth. Immediately her treacherous mind began to fill with images of what would be happening during the silences.

She recalled the swift bruising kiss he had given her in the restaurant. And though she longed to hurl some caustic retort at him, the words simply wouldn't come.

What would it be like to feel those lips stray over her body in warm and tender exploration?

And his hands, so strong and capable with the sails, yet so light on the wheel. What would they feel like gliding over her bare skin? She swallowed, forcing the enchanting, tormenting images out of her mind.

'Of course, I wouldn't have that problem with you, would I?' he said softly.

'*You* wouldn't have *any* problems with me,' Polly snapped, glaring at him, her chin high.

He said nothing, simply raising his eyebrows.

She groaned inaudibly, and wished the deck would open up and swallow her.

What she had meant was that there was absolutely no chance of her joining his lists of conquests. But he had interpreted her remark to mean exactly the opposite.

Explanations would only make matters ten times worse. In any case, how could she look into his eyes and convince him she wouldn't touch him with a ten-foot pole when every time he came within a few feet of her she quivered inside, remembering the fierce and all too brief pressure of his mouth on hers?

A public kiss, it had been fleeting. And despite what he'd said, less a token of affection than a means of throwing her off balance. Yet the sensation was indelibly stamped on her memory. And to her shame she longed to feel it again.

Her face on fire, she looked at her watch. 'Lord, is that the time? I'd better get lunch.'

'Running away, little girl?' he taunted softly.

Polly tilted her chin, rage at his cruel teasing lending her courage. 'Take a look in the mirror, Nathan Bryce.'

He was suddenly still. 'What?'

'Nothing. Forget it. You take the wheel, I'm going——'

He stood up, blocking her escape. 'You're going nowhere until you explain.'

Polly moistened her lips. 'A different woman every day?' Her brows arched and she shook her head. 'It doesn't take a psychologist to see that it's *you* who's running.'

'Now hang on a minute,' he snapped. 'Most of the women I'm photographed with are simply social acquaintances.'

'Is *that* what you call it?' Polly retorted, throwing his own words back at him.

His features tightened. 'As for being my "constant companion", most of the time I don't even know their names.'

'Please!' With an expression of pained distaste Polly closed her eyes briefly to silence him. 'The sordid details of your liaisons are of no interest to me.'

Nathan's look as he towered over her sent cold shivers rippling down her spine. 'That's strange,' he mused softly. 'I got the distinct impression you were jealous.'

'Jealous? Me?' Polly laughed, and wished it sounded more convincing.

'Well, you do seem to be remarkably interested in my love life.'

'*Love* is not the word I'd use to describe your activities,' Polly said caustically. 'And as for being jealous, you've got to be joking.' She glared at him, trying to project pity, annoyance, and exasperation all at the same time. 'Isn't that just typical? I make an observation about a recurring item in a newspaper and you interpret it as jealousy.' She shook her head. 'Talk about vain.'

His gaze travelled over her face, and the look in his eyes made her ache inside. 'So much fire,' he murmured. 'You really are beautiful when you're angry.'

'And you're a walking cliché,' Polly retorted, her cheeks scalding hot. It was definitely time to put some space between them. 'I'm going to get lunch. Will sandwiches and coffee suit you?'

'Is there a choice?'

'Not if you want *me* to prepare it.'

'That's what you're here for. At least,' he added, making her stomach knot, 'it's one of the reasons.'

Before she could respond he continued, 'Sandwiches and coffee will be fine. I'll eat anything provided someone else gets it ready. I'm not the world's greatest cook.'

'That's hardly surprising,' Polly retorted. 'In fact,' she delivered the shaft of a sweet smile, 'I wonder you even find time to eat.'

'God, woman,' Nathan's eyes glittered dangerously, 'you do push your luck.'

With a brisk nod Polly relinquished the wheel and dived down the companionway. Bracing herself against the movement of the boat, she clutched the crash bar in front of the cooker with one hand and pressed the other to her face. Her cheeks were burning and her heart hammered against her ribs as though trying to escape. She felt elated and furious, and trembled with nervous energy.

She could hardly believe what she'd just done. Never in her entire life had she spoken to anyone the way she had just spoken to Nathan Bryce. But it was his own fault. He had asked for it.

Rinsing her hands with cold water, she splashed some on her face. She had to get a grip on herself. There was no denying he was an exceptionally attractive man. But responding to Nathan Bryce's flirting was about as wise as striking matches to find a gas leak.

He knew all the moves. He had probably invented them. She, on the other hand, was in unknown territory. Giles had hurt her badly. Now, when she looked back, she couldn't help wondering—had she really loved him? She had thought so at the time. But if someone loved you, how could they treat you so cruelly? Yet Giles was a lamb compared to the wolfish cunning of Nathan Bryce.

Polly poured the steaming coffee into a vacuum jug and wrapped the plate of cheese and tomato sandwiches lightly in clingfilm. Then, taking two mugs from the cupboard, she spooned sugar into hers and carried the lot carefully up the ladder.

Sitting in one corner of the moulded seat which ran round three sides of the cockpit, she bit into a sandwich, suddenly ravenous. Nathan was seated in the opposite corner, one hand easy on the wheel as he helped himself from the plate.

Gazing out over the water, the sun hot on her bare limbs, Polly sighed and allowed herself to relax.

'Though this isn't what I'd have chosen,' Nathan murmured, 'I have to admit there are worse ways of spending a few weeks. So much of my time is spent designing or in meetings it's all too easy to forget that this,' he gazed around him, 'is the purpose of it all.'

'Mmm.' Polly refused to comment. In one sense he was right; the trip itself was a wonderful change from her daily routine too. But having him as her only companion meant she had to be constantly on her guard. Against her own treacherous thoughts as much as against him.

'We'll take on fresh food and water when we reach Ibiza,' Nathan announced.

'How far is that?' Eyes closed, Polly was enjoying the warm breeze ruffling her hair.

'About four hundred and thirty miles.' She heard him reach for another sandwich.

'Surely we can't do that distance in a day?'

Nathan laughed. '*Seawitch* is fast, but not *that* fast. It'll probably take us two and a half.'

Polly looked across at him, feeling a twinge of unease. 'So where will we be anchoring overnight?'

His brows climbed. 'We won't. Surely you realised that? Apart from taking on essential supplies, the trip is non-stop. We'll take turns on watch.'

Her appetite vanished. In fact, she felt decidedly queasy. Returning her half-eaten sandwich to the plate, she picked up her mug, hoping the hot coffee would force the lump of half-chewed food down her suddenly constricted throat.

Nathan scanned the sky. 'It looks as if we might be in for a bit of a blow,' he remarked.

Polly tipped her head back. A thin veil of high cloud had made the sun hazy. The jaunty white puffs had become ragged and dirty grey. The sea had lost its sparkle and now looked leaden and lumpy. Her stomach lurched. The change had been so sudden. Even the breeze had a keener edge.

Nathan stood up. 'I'm going to shorten sail.' He indicated the tray. 'You get that lot below and break out the wet-weather gear. The oilskins locker is in the passage behind the chart table. Put on a sweater, and bring me one as well. Move yourself, girl,' he rapped. 'Things happen fast out here at this time of year.'

Clive had warned her. But with temperatures in the high sixties, a gentle breeze, and uninterrupted sunshine from a cornflower-blue sky, she hadn't believed him.

Heart pounding, Polly stumbled one-handed down the companionway and dumped mugs, flask, and the plate containing the last few sandwiches in the nearer sink.

Below deck the boat's movement seemed more pronounced. Lurching through the saloon into her own cabin, she grabbed a sweater from the locker beneath her berth and slammed the cabin door behind her.

Tugging the sweater on over her head as she hurried aft, she told herself there was absolutely nothing to be afraid of. Having designed and built this boat, Nathan knew its capabilities better than anyone. Besides, he was one of the world's top yachtsmen. So if it was going to get rough she couldn't be in safer hands.

Nathan Bryce *safe*? Who was she trying to kid? All she was interested in right now, she told herself firmly as she banished tantalising, *dangerous* thoughts concerning those strong brown hands, was his ability to keep them afloat.

In the passage she wrenched open the locker and hauled the oilskins off their hangers.

'Polly,' Nathan shouted down the companionway, 'while you're down there, close the hatches.'

Dumping the oilskins on the floor, she fastened the saloon deck hatch, then hurried to his cabin and fastened that hatch. She was already on her way out when she remembered his sweater. She found one, shut the locker and the cabin door, scooped up the oilskins, and scrambled up the companionway into the cockpit.

Nathan was still on the coach roof lashing the reefed mainsail to stop it chafing.

As she struggled into the stiff shiny yellow jacket and leggings, obviously made for someone twice her size, Nathan jumped down into the cockpit. He slid the companionway hatch cover forward and fastened the doors, shutting off the interior of the yacht.

Watching as he pulled on his oilskins with an ease born of long practice, Polly shivered violently. Isolated in this small square well in the deck, they were exposed to anything the elements cared to throw at them.

Nathan tossed her a safety harness. 'Get that on, then take the wheel. There are a couple of things I want to do before it reaches us.'

Polly pushed her arms through the webbing straps that reminded her of the restrainer her eldest sister used to stop her adventurous offspring clambering out of their prams and buggies. Her throat was so dry that it hurt. 'Before what reaches us?' she croaked, hanging on to the wheel as if it were a lifebelt.

Nathan jerked a thumb over his shoulder. 'That.'

CHAPTER SIX

POLLY glanced round. Her eyes widened in horror as she saw the straight black line of a squall bearing down on them.

'Watch your course,' Nathan yelled, seizing the wheel from her and turning it as *Seawitch* lost the wind and wallowed. The headsail flapped uselessly, snaking and snapping the ropes.

'S-sorry,' Polly stammered above the wind. Off balance and staggering, she grabbed for a hand-hold.

Taking one hand off the wheel, Nathan reached out and hooked his fingers through the front of her harness. Polly caught her breath, instinctively jerking backwards away from him. But he didn't let go.

'Don't you think this might be more effective if it was attached to something?' he enquired acidly, indicating a stainless steel anchorage point.

'I——' she started, but bit the words off. She was supposed to be an experienced sailor. How could she tell him she'd never used one before? 'I've only got two hands, and you——' A strange hissing sound made her look over her shoulder.

A wall of water extended from the heavy black cloud to the sea, which frothed, briefly flattened by the force of the deluge. The huge drops were so close together that they reflected the light, and the rain billowed and rippled like a silver-white curtain.

The hiss was followed by a roar as a sudden burst of wind hit them, hurling *Seawitch* forward like a blow from a giant fist.

Spume was whipped from heaving pewter-grey waves. The punishing rain made it difficult even to breathe. Mixed with spray, it streamed over Polly's face and ran in cold trickles down her neck. Her hair was plastered to her scalp, and she had to keep blinking and wiping her eyes in order to see at all.

Nathan kept shouting orders at her. But he might have been speaking a foreign language.

'For God's sake, girl, stop dithering,' he roared, impatience turning rapidly to anger.

Mountains of foam-streaked grey water humped and dipped all around them as *Seawitch* porpoised through the broken waves. The roller-coaster movement was distinctly uncomfortable, and Polly's stomach began to rebel.

'The wind's backing,' Nathan shouted across.

How on earth could he tell? she wondered, hunched against the banshee howling that came at her from all directions, hurling rain against her skin with such force it stung like grit. And what did it mean?

'Get ready to come about.'

She glanced in dismayed confusion at the array of winches, then up at him in desperate appeal. 'I don't— I can't——' she shrugged hopelessly.

His brief puzzled frown hardened into furious realisation. 'First that one,' he rasped, pointing, 'then those two.' His jaw was set like chiselled granite. Rain ran down the harsh planes of his face and dripped from his chin on to the slick oilskin. His narrowed eyes were dagger-bright.

Polly looked away, her stomach churning with a nausea that couldn't be blamed solely on hunger or seasickness.

Nathan spun the wheel and *Seawitch* changed direction. As he loosed the mainsheet the sail swung across to its new position.

Polly worked swiftly, hauling in and securing the various ropes. She focused all her concentration on getting it right, not daring to look at Nathan, or even to think about what would happen next.

The lurching and corkscrewing stopped and the boat sliced more smoothly through the turbulent water. Polly slumped down on the moulded seat. Stretching her arms out on either side to steady herself, she clung to the edge of the cockpit. She was shaking all over, partly from cold, partly from shock at the suddenness and ferocity of the squall, but mostly in anticipation of what was to come.

She had realised the moment he walked into the Customs office that Nathan Bryce was not a man to cross. But when she had made her reckless decision to sail with him, it had never occurred to her that the smooth, sunny Mediterranean of holiday brochures might have a darker, more dangerous face. Now her plan to bluff her way through had been reduced to a pitiful shambles.

As quickly as it had arrived, the squall passed. The rain ceased as if a tap had been turned off. The wind dropped from a screaming, gusting gale to a fresh breeze.

And as she raised her chilled, dripping face to look at the sky, the black clouds parted. Golden rays beamed down like spotlights, transforming the charcoal water to sapphire-blue and making the streaks of foam sparkle like sugar frosting.

The squall moved rapidly away, fading into the distance like a memory, leaving behind it crystal-clear air and a freshly washed sky the colour of forget-me-nots. The deck was already beginning to dry and for

Polly the sun's luxuriant warmth on her soaked head was like a blessing. But the wet clammy oilskins were beginning to resemble a sauna.

As she fumbled with trembling fingers at the clip on her safety harness she could feel Nathan's gaze burning into her.

'How much sailing did you say you'd done?' he enquired in that soft even tone she knew to be lethal.

Polly tried to suppress the shudder that galvanised every nerve from the roots of her hair to her toes and fingertips. His very quietness terrified her. She swallowed. 'I didn't.' Her voice was husky. She was surrounded by water, yet her mouth was as dry as the Sahara.

'You *have* sailed before.' His tone made the words a statement which merely required confirmation. Polly took a deep breath and shook her head.

His gaze pierced her like cold steel. 'But you told me——'

'I told you I could *cook*,' she broke in. 'It was as a cook that I was sailing with Clive.'

'You have never crewed on a yacht?'

Moistening her lips, Polly shook her head. 'Clive said he didn't need a crew, only someone to take care of the meals——' She drew her palm across her forehead. She was sweating, yet her skin felt cold. Rainwater dribbled down her temples and the back of her neck.

Beneath his tan Nathan was pale with fury. 'You lied to me.' He ground the words out through gritted teeth.

Polly had never been so frightened in her life. Given the choice, she would rather have faced the squall again.

'I didn't,' she defied him, her voice thin. 'I never

claimed to be an experienced sailor. You simply *assumed* I was.'

'Well, if you're not, what the hell are you doing on my boat?' he roared.

Oddly, his loss of temper was a relief to Polly. She could cope with that, whereas his icy controlled quietness petrified her.

'The alternative was gaol. Remember?' she shouted back. 'I preferred to take my chances out here.'

'You stupid, pea-brained *idiot*,' he stormed. 'This isn't a pleasure trip——'

'You can say that again,' she hurled the words at him. '*Pleasure* is the last word I'd associate with your company.'

Fear, attraction, dismay, and total confusion: she had experienced them all since meeting him the previous day. But not pleasure. That was far too weak and mild a word for the emotions he stirred. Her stomach lurched and she wiped her forehead again.

His eyes narrowed. 'What's the matter?'

'Nothing. I'm fine,' she snapped. In fact she felt awful, nauseous and light-headed and clammy. More than anything in the world she wanted to lie down. Maybe if she could just curl up on her bed and sleep for a while she'd feel better. But she'd bite her tongue off sooner than ask *him* for any favours.

'Get below,' he ordered.

'I'm perfectly all right,' she began.

'If you feel as sick as you look, you most certainly are not *all right*,' he retorted.

Oddly, it wasn't his anger that made her eyes prickle and her vision blur. It was the totally unexpected sympathy tempering his exasperation as he said, 'Go and lie down, Polly.'

Furious that a rare kind word from Nathan Bryce

could so easily demolish the façade of efficiency and confidence she had worked so desperately hard to maintain, she blinked hard and sucked in a deep breath. She must not, *would* not give way now. Ironically, his next words gave her spine just the stiffening it needed.

'I need time to decide what to do with you,' he mused—then added darkly, 'At this precise moment heaving you overboard has its attractions.'

Polly's head flew up. Tears forgotten, she gasped. 'You——'

'*Wouldn't dare*?' His narrowed eyes glittered. 'Don't bet on it.' He turned his head away. 'And I was beginning to think you were different,' he muttered, his tone full of self-mockery. His brief laugh was a harsh, tearing sound. 'But you're not. You're just like all the rest.'

'All what rest?' she demanded blankly. 'I don't know what you're talking about.'

'No, of course you don't.' The cutting scorn that hardened his eyes and thinned his mouth made her flinch.

Then she realised. 'How dare you? I'm not the least bit like the fleet of models and would-be actresses the Press politely call your *constant companions*. But even if I were, what right have you to be so disappointed? After all, you chose them. Nobody held a gun to your head.'

Pushing unpainted fingers through her cropped chestnut curls, she looked down, and thought of her own boyishly slender figure beneath the enveloping oilskins.

'I wasn't referring to physical appearance,' he snapped.

She flushed. 'You couldn't be, as I'm neither blonde

nor shaped like an hourglass. And as the kind of girls you seem to prefer would think a job like mine utterly boring, I don't see how you can possibly say I'm just like them. I'm not *just like* anyone. I'm me.' She broke off, breathless, confused, and feeling worse than ever.

'Yes,' he snarled. 'And you wouldn't recognise truth if it jumped up and bit you. You lied about being able to sail.' His face was a taut bitter mask. 'Did you lie about the drugs too?'

Anguish overwhelmed her. '*No!*' she cried. 'Nathan, please, you have to believe me——'

'Get below, Polly,' he repeated with soft, tightly reined violence, and turned away.

Though something told her his fury was greater than her deception over her sailing experience warranted, Polly felt too ill to force the issue by demanding explanations. She went.

At the bottom of the companionway she struggled out of the wet oilskins and dropped them on the floor in a heap. They were quickly followed by her damp jumper.

Sweating and shivering, she stumbled through the saloon to her cabin. Pulling a fresh towel from her locker, she wiped her face, neck and throat, and gave her head a quick rub. Then, tossing the towel to one side, she closed her eyes and collapsed on to the open sleeping-bag.

Her cheek touched cold *wet* cotton. She frowned, hazily exploring the area near her face with one hand.

Her eyes flew open and she reared back, scrambling to her feet. The sleeping-bag was soaked. She explored further. So were the pillows, and the mattress.

Leaning against the door, she forced her weary fuddled brain to work. *How*? As realisation broke over her like a drenching wave her whole body sagged.

The hatches. She had closed all the others but, busy trying to remember Nathan's list of instructions, she had forgotten hers. And as it couldn't be seen from the cockpit there had been nothing to remind her that it was still open.

Feeling more wretched than ever, she stumbled out of her cabin. She couldn't possibly sleep there. She'd probably die of pneumonia, if Nathan didn't throw her overboard first. And he had even more reason to now.

Dragging two musty-smelling blankets from the storage locker outside her door, she left one folded up as a pillow, shook the other one out and wrapped it around her, then lay down on one of the settees which provided seating and converted to pilot-berths on either side of the drop-leaf dining table.

The relief was indescribable. She was still shivering and her head felt muzzy, but now she was lying down the boat didn't seem to be doing quite so much heaving and rolling. Nor did her stomach.

Gradually the shivering stopped and her muscles began to relax. She began to drift and was just dozing off when she heard the squeak of Nathan's deck shoes on the ladder.

Fearing the worst, Polly jerked upright, wild-eyed and blinking. 'What's the matter? What's gone wrong?' Her voice emerged, cracked and husky, from a throat tight with dread. 'Who's sailing the boat?'

Startled, clearly not expecting to see her there, Nathan dumped his own oilskins and sweater on top of hers. 'Nothing's wrong,' he replied curtly. 'At least, not with the boat.' The teeming rain had run down his neck and soaked the top half of his T-shirt, which clung damply. Hooking the shirt off over his dripping head, he dropped it on to the pile. Then, taking the towel from the rail in front of the cooker, he wiped his face, head and forearms.

Polly watched him. Tall, broad-shouldered, with lean hips and muscular legs, he was magnificent to look at. He was also formidable, demanding, difficult—and smouldering with anger, but she still found it impossible to tear her gaze away.

'*Seawitch* is on auto-pilot.' Flipping the towel over his shoulder, he raked his fingers through his spikily tousled hair a couple of times, restoring it to rough order. Starting towards his cabin, he stopped and turned back, frowning.

'What are you doing out here?' he demanded. 'Why aren't you in your cabin?'

As the boat lurched Polly sat down suddenly, clasping her hands tightly together. She knew it was useless to lie.

Swallowing, she moistened her lips. 'My sleeping-bag and mattress got wet. I forgot to close the deck hatch when the squall——' Her voice tailed off and she moved her shoulders briefly. 'I'm sorry,' she whispered.

His features tightened. 'Of all the stupid, careless——' Flinching beneath contemptuous anger that gave each word the force of a blow, Polly could only watch as he made a visible effort to control himself. 'You were right,' he gritted. 'You're unique. In a class of your own.'

She bit her lip. He wasn't paying her a compliment.

His gaze swept over her from head to foot. It was impossible to guess from his narrowed eyes and set features what he was thinking. Did she look as bad as she felt? Leaping up like that had brought back the awful queasiness.

'Obviously, lying down hasn't helped much,' he observed. 'Have you been sick?'

Miserably, she shook her head. She almost wished she could be. Anything would be better than feeling like this.

'In that case, work is the answer,' he announced briskly. 'You can start by cleaning up that mess.' He indicated the sink.

Swallowing, Polly looked up at him, wretched but defiant. 'Are you punishing me?'

His gaze softened. 'For feeling seasick? Of course not. But keeping busy really is the best cure. It takes your mind off how you feel. Besides,' his features underwent a subtle change, setting to granite hardness, 'I paid your bail because I needed a crew as well as a cook. And seasick or not, you're going to honour your end of the deal.'

Polly moistened her lips. 'What exactly do you mean by that?' She hated the quaver in her voice. But just at that moment, standing tall and bronzed in nothing but a pair of ragged denim shorts, his black hair tumbling damply across his forehead, Nathan Bryce did not fit the expected image of a millionaire yacht designer.

'Pirate' was the word that leapt into Polly's mind as she stared helplessly at him.

'I mean that, among other things, you're going to learn to sail. And you're going to learn fast. If you want to eat, that is,' he added with quiet menace.

Polly opened her mouth, and closed it again quickly. Already she knew him well enough to realise he would never make threats he wasn't prepared to carry out.

Never in her life had she felt less like eating than she did at this moment. But if she didn't try, or he refused her food because she wouldn't do as he told her, she would quickly become too weak. Too weak for what? To get away. She hadn't even realised the thought was in her mind until this moment. Her best chance would come when they reached Ibiza in two days' time.

'So,' Nathan pulled the towel from his shoulder and tossed it aside, 'after you've tidied the galley, wipe the oilskins dry and hang them in the locker. When you've done that, open the saloon deck hatch and put the sweaters on hangers, then hook them over the coaming. That's the raised rim around the hatch that keeps the water out,' he explained as if talking to a three-year-old. 'Then bring your sleeping-bag up on deck. And your mattress. They'll take days to dry, so the sooner you get them into the sun the better. And then make us both a hot drink. Do you think you can remember all that, or shall I write it down?'

Polly's flaring anger at his sarcasm was quickly extinguished by a far more pressing question. She screwed up her courage. 'You aren't going to take me back to Gibraltar?'

He gazed at her in silence for several seconds, then replied with icy simplicity, 'No time. You lied your way on to this voyage by implying you were an experienced crew. And that's exactly what you're going to become.' A momentary pause gave his final words chilling emphasis. 'No matter what it takes.'

As he strode off to his cabin Polly sank down on the settee, wondering how she was going to survive. She felt sick and shivery. Her head was thumping, and her damp shirt was sticking to her. What was she doing here?

Would she rather be in gaol?

At least there the floor would be still, and she wouldn't be feeling so horribly queasy, and she'd have a dry bed.

The sound of Nathan's returning footsteps brought her swiftly and instinctively to her feet. She reached down to pick up the sweater she had thrown on to her own oilskins.

Tucking a clean pale blue T-shirt into his shorts, he didn't even glance in her direction, but called over his shoulder as he hoisted himself up the ladder, 'I'll expect a mug of tea in five minutes.'

'Yes, master,' she muttered, glaring at his bronzed legs as they disappeared through the hatch.

As she lurched her way to the galley and filled the kettle, anger seethed through her. Nathan Bryce might have a temporary advantage, but no slate-eyed, ruthless, mercenary businessman with a calculator instead of a heart was going to get the better of *her*.

Lighting the gas, she secured the kettle within the rails which would hold it in place, then snatched up the dishcloth. Spreading the oilskins out on the floor, she wiped them off, finishing the process with the towel Nathan had tossed on to the worktop.

As she hung the waterproofs in the locker she remembered with vivid clarity how his gaze had met hers after Giles had been led away by the stewards.

Since then she had seen many different expressions in his eyes: amusement, surprise, speculation, even respect. But contempt had returned with a vengeance, erasing everything else the moment he realised she didn't know what to do when he changed the boat's direction.

He had written her off as a useless, lying bimbo. Well, she was going to show him just how wrong he was. She could almost be grateful for the experience with Giles. For she was wiser now and stronger. Quite strong enough to deal with a man like Nathan Bryce.

A shudder ran through her as she suddenly remembered one very valid point. With Giles she had been able to turn her back and walk away.

She couldn't walk off a boat in mid-ocean. She had to keep going until they reached Ibiza. The next few days would test her nerve to the limit.

The kettle began to whistle, breaking into her train of thought. She looked around, surprised. She had been so immersed in her anger and indignation that she had been working on automatic pilot herself. The sweaters hung beneath the open hatch, the sink was empty and the oilskins stowed away.

She took Nathan's tea up and, at his insistence, returned to fetch her own.

'If you're going to be of any use to me at all, the work has to start now.'

She simply nodded, but her heart sank at the prospect implied by his cold clipped tones. Reality was even worse. For the rest of that day and evening Nathan kept her constantly busy. When she wasn't preparing food she could barely swallow, or making hot drinks, or washing up, he was instructing her on how to use the boat's equipment. Then he would test her to make sure she was taking it in.

By ten that evening Polly was literally reeling with exhaustion. When Nathan ordered her to set up and engage the auto-helm she tried, desperately searching a mind that had gone totally blank for the sequence which would ensure that the boat remained on course. But it was hopeless.

'I'm sorry.' She pressed her fingertips to her temples, shaking her head. 'I can't remember.' Shoulders bowed, almost drunk with fatigue, she waited for his scathing tirade.

'Go and get some sleep,' he said at last, his voice devoid of expression.

As the words sank in she raised her head. 'I'll do better tomorrow.' She was careful to match his lack of expression. It wouldn't do to let him see her relief and gratitude.

He gazed past her. The pale glow from the masthead light emphasised his strong profile while deepening the shadows around his eyes. 'Take my cabin.'

She looked at him quickly, but he gave her no chance to reply.

'Don't waste time arguing.' His tone was brusque. 'You're hardly an asset now. Without proper rest you'll be a positive liability.'

Various responses chased across her tongue, but Polly swallowed them all. Unfortunately he was right. She ached in every muscle from the constant strain of trying to keep her balance on the heaving deck. And, though she was tired enough to sleep on a clothes-line, the chance to spread her weary limbs over the full width of a double mattress instead of lying cramped on the narrow settee was too appealing to turn down.

'Thank you,' she managed finally. 'Goodnight.'

His only reply was a grunt.

At the top of the ladder she hesitated. 'Nathan?'

'What?' His tone was not encouraging.

'I swear I've told you the truth about the drugs. I really didn't know.'

His eyes were ice-bright, and pierced her like twin blades as he regarded her for a long moment. 'Go to bed,' he said, turning away.

Polly stumbled down the ladder. Her brain felt like scrambled egg. She craved the oblivion of sleep, desperate to escape the physical discomfort and mental exhaustion which had worsened as the day had worn on.

Yet nausea and bone-weariness were mere pinpricks

compared to the emotional upheaval she was going through. Though she tried to tell herself it didn't matter whether or not he believed her, *she* knew the truth—it did. It mattered terribly. And, because of what had happened to his father, honesty and integrity were of far greater importance to him than to many businessmen she had worked for.

With cool detachment he had explained clearly and in terms that were easy for her to grasp how the various items of equipment worked, only lapsing into irritation or sarcasm when he thought she was not making enough effort.

'We both know you've got a brain. Try using it.'

Such remarks, though a backhanded compliment in their implied assumption of her intelligence, made her hate him with such an intensity that she could actually feel herself start to tremble and sweat. 'Please,' she demurred through gritted teeth, 'no flattery.'

Yet despite the antagonism that vibrated between them, Polly still found him profoundly attractive. It was as if he exerted some kind of gravitational pull over her.

Clearly it wasn't deliberate. His manner made it obvious he didn't like her. Well, she didn't like him either. So why did she feel so irresistibly drawn to him? It was appalling and ridiculous, and this inner battle was draining away what little strength she had left.

For the first time in her adult life, Polly went to bed without bathing or cleaning her teeth. She stripped to her panties, crawled into the sleeping-bag, and lapsed into unconsciousness as her head touched the pillow.

Waking with a start, she lay in the grey half-light of dawn, wondering where she was. Then as memory returned she closed her eyes, her sigh ending in a groan.

The sound of footsteps on the deck above her head brought her fully awake. Nathan must have been on deck all night. Not only on deck, but on watch. He would not have risked their safety in the busy Mediterranean shipping lanes by sleeping.

She jumped out of bed and, pulling on her shirt, darted next door into the head.

Emerging a quarter of an hour later, showered, her hair washed and teeth cleaned, she felt very much better. Eight hours of deep, dreamless sleep had helped enormously. Apart from a slight queasiness, physically she felt quite fit. For which she was very grateful when she thought of what the day ahead was likely to hold.

Work-wise it followed a similar pattern to the previous day. But if Nathan had been difficult then, today he was virtually impossible. Terse and abrupt, the orders he issued took almost no account of her lack of experience.

Polly battled on, practically biting her tongue in half. She tried to make allowances, constantly reminding herself of the responsibility Nathan was carrying and how long he had been without sleep.

As the day wore on her nerves grew more and more frayed. After yet another bawling-out following their evening meal, which once again she had hardly been able to touch, Nathan sent her below to make coffee. 'Perhaps a shot of caffeine will stir your grey cells into some sort of life,' he snapped. 'What is it about boats that makes women so inept?'

'I'm doing my best,' she blazed back. 'Before yesterday I didn't even know port from starboard. I've learned more in twenty-four hours than most people would manage in a week. Yet all you can do is carp and criticise. Well, I've had enough.' Turning her back on his icy gaze, she stormed down the ladder.

But out of sight in the galley, she gripped the rail in front of the cooker to steady herself and choked back tears of rage and frustration. He was absolutely impossible.

'Where the hell's that coffee?' Nathan roared down the hatch.

Polly lifted her chin. She'd taken as much from him as she was going to. Wiping her tear-streaked face with the back of her hand, she yelled back, 'Where the hell do you think? I'm waiting for the beans to ripen. If you want it any faster, come and make it yourself.'

She held her breath, tensed against the tongue-lashing she was sure would come. Only it didn't. Not a word.

Though relieved, and fiercely delighted that she had apparently stopped him in his tracks, Polly was apprehensive about going back up on deck.

When she finally appeared and handed Nathan his mug he nodded coolly. After taking a sip he glanced across to where she was sitting.

'Starting tonight you'll stand a watch. You can take the four hours from two a.m. until six.'

Polly stared at him, filled with a mixture of pride and terror. He wouldn't put her on watch if he didn't think she could handle the responsibility. On the other hand, it was obvious from the shadows like sooty thumbprints beneath his eyes and the tension around his mouth that he desperately needed some sleep. With only the two of them on board his choices were limited.

Determined to respond in the same offhand manner

with which he had made the announcement, she simply
tossed her head. 'OK.'

But as she raised the mug to her lips her hand shook
and, instead of the sip she had intended to take, she
ended up gulping and burned her mouth.

She shot him a quick, embarrassed glance. But to
her untold relief he seemed preoccupied and obviously
hadn't noticed. Lord only knew what cutting com-
ments would have come her way if he had.

She took another careful sip. This time when she
looked up he was watching her.

'So,' he said, 'as soon as you've finished your coffee,
I want you in bed.'

The words vibrated in the air between them like the
aftermath of an explosion. His swift intake of breath
and the shock that flashed across his face mirrored her
own as their eyes locked in a split-second of naked
honesty.

Polly's heart pounded like a hammer in her ears.
Nathan gave a brief shrug, and a wry, self-mocking
smile flickered at the corners of his mouth.

'How about that for a Freudian slip?' he murmured.

Flushing from her toes to the roots of her hair, Polly
drained the last of her coffee, the mug clattering
against her teeth. She stood up.

Immediately Nathan rose too, casually placing himself between her and the companionway. Silhouetted
by the masthead light above, and the glow from the
saloon, he loomed, dark and threatening, against the
night sky.

Polly swallowed. 'Don't let it worry you.'

'It doesn't,' he assured her.

'I know you couldn't possibly have meant it.'

'Oh? Why not?' He was being deliberately awkward
and provocative.

'Because,' Polly said crisply, 'you've just spent the entire day yelling at me, and telling me how slow, clumsy, and generally useless I am.'

'So?' he demanded. 'Why should that make any difference?'

'Are you serious?' she flared. 'When you look at me it's usually with contempt. You refuse to accept that I knew nothing about the drugs. You accuse me of being "just like all the rest", which is clearly an insult. And,' her blush deepened, 'you're obviously determined to believe the worst of me where both Giles and Clive are concerned.' Her nails bit into her palms as she hurled all her anger and bitter hurt at him. 'In the circumstances, how could you possibly want to go to bed with someone like me?'

The silence stretched, broken only by the slap of the water against the hull and Polly's heart thundering in her ears.

'How indeed?' he mused ironically. 'But I do.'

Polly caught her breath as she drew herself up. Every sinew in her slender frame radiated defiance. 'I'm worth more than that, Nathan Bryce.' Her whole stance was a silent challenge to him to deny it, but she had to press her lips tightly together to stop them quivering.

Slowly he raised one hand and gently cupped her face.

Polly wanted to jerk away, but her body refused to obey her brain's command. The warmth from his palm curled through her like smoke. It comforted, soothed, excited and terrified.

She swallowed, her heart leaping wildly. His head came down. She couldn't move. She felt his warm breath on her cheek. 'Yes,' he murmured, his lips brushing hers, a touch as light as a moth's wing.

Her eyes closed, Polly stopped breathing. Yes what? Yes, she was worth more? She wanted—wanted—what? *Him*. His mouth covered hers and time seemed to stand still. For several blissful seconds she abandoned herself to his kiss, and to all the incredible, startling sensations exploding inside her. Then she froze. What was she doing?

Her hands flew up, pushing against the wall of his chest. And, with a gasp, she freed herself, stumbling backwards, her head bent as she struggled against the hunger and disappointment that clamoured inside her.

'What's your price, Polly?' Nathan grated.

Stunned, she gaped at him. '*What*?'

'Come on,' he rapped impatiently. 'What are you holding out for?'

'I don't know what you mean,' she cried, hugging her arms across her chest, shaken by the bleakness of his expression and the loathing in his eyes.

'Yes, you do.' His lethal smile made her skin crawl. 'I'm talking about sex. When a man wants a woman he pays, one way or another.'

Polly stared at him, trembling with anger and humiliation. 'Do you *really* believe that?' Her voice was a husky rasp. 'Nathan Bryce, I feel terribly sorry for you.'

It was Nathan's turn to look shocked. Then his face grew thunderous. 'You *what*?'

Polly swallowed. 'You've probably had more. . .' she flushed '. . .sex than I've had hot dinners. But obviously you've never known love. I think that's very sad.'

'Don't patronise me, young woman,' Nathan roared.

She flinched. 'I'm not. I——'

'And what makes you such an expert on love?' he demanded, cutting across her attempt to explain.

'Giles Denton's reputation springs from the number, not the quality or duration of his. . .liaisons.'

Wincing as the shaft struck home, Polly stiffened. 'Rather like yours,' she retaliated.

They glared at one another, attraction and antagonism crackling between them like electricity.

Suddenly he reached for her. Startled, she jerked backwards, her breath catching in her throat. But the cockpit was too small. There was nowhere to go.

Grasping her upper arms, he pulled her hard against him. His roughness, hinting at violent emotions barely controlled, made her frighteningly aware of his awesome strength. Yet when his mouth claimed hers once more, there was pleading in the passion that made her head spin, and she responded instinctively. Her lips parted to admit the hot, sweet lance of his tongue. She felt his breath on her face, heard the low sound in his throat and knew that, in spite of the terrible confusion he aroused in her, she didn't want this moment to end.

Tearing his mouth from hers, Nathan thrust her away. They were both breathing fast, and Polly's legs threatened to give way at any second.

Nathan grabbed his empty coffee-mug and pushed it into her unsteady hand, turning aside. 'Go and get some sleep.' His tone was curt, his voice slightly hoarse.

'I——' She had to clear her throat and start again. 'About my turn on watch. I—I'm afraid I don't have an alarm.'

'No matter.' Busy checking the compass, he didn't look at her. 'I'll wake you when it's time.'

She nodded. 'Thank you.' She started down the companionway. 'Goodnight.'

He didn't answer.

CHAPTER SEVEN

AFTER rinsing the mugs and putting them away, Polly staggered through the saloon to her own cabin to fetch her night attire, a pair of jeans, and her Aran cardigan. She washed quickly and brushed her teeth, then returned to Nathan's cabin.

Though closing the door shut her off from the rest of the boat, she was still acutely aware of him only inches away on the other side of the deckhead.

As she undressed she saw her limbs were rainbowed with bruises from bumping into various bits of furniture. Pulling on the soft, baggy shirt she slept in, she sat on the bed and massaged her legs. The muscles ached with the strain of trying to balance on the constantly shifting deck. Life on a yacht, even one as well equipped as this, was far more physically demanding than she had ever imagined. If only her stomach would settle and she could face eating again perhaps she would feel less tired and her nerves less ragged.

Sighing, she swivelled round, looking at the cabin properly for the first time. The varnished wood, pale cream paintwork and maroon fabric were the same as in her own cabin.

But whereas the shelf above her bed was empty, this one was crammed with books. As she scanned the titles Polly's brows contracted in a puzzled frown.

The clutch of recent paperback thrillers was no great surprise to her. Nor were the textbooks on engineering, navigation, physics, and design technology. They went with the notebooks and perspex box containing drawing instruments and a slide rule sitting in the open top of the bedside locker.

But she certainly hadn't expected to see a selection of Penguin Classics. Or the works of Charles Dickens sandwiched between a well-thumbed leather-bound edition of the Romantic poets and three volumes of philosophy.

Polly rubbed the back of her neck, hoping to soothe away the tightness before it became a headache. Something didn't add up. If this was a true reflection of Nathan Bryce's personality and taste, how had he acquired such a totally different public image?

Like the rest of the boat, the cabin had been fitted out to a high standard using top-quality materials. But there was certainly no overt luxury. It was basic and functional rather than hedonistic.

True, the mattress was much larger than hers. But then it would need to be for a man of his size to stretch out in comfort. *With someone else*?

Polly tried to tell herself it was none of her business. Though it would certainly be in keeping with his media image if he were to use *Seawitch* for what the tabloids liked to call a 'love nest'.

Yet he had made no secret of his opinion that women and boats were about as compatible as oil and water. And the cabin's ambience reinforced that view. In fact there was something almost monastic about it: as if it were a retreat for much needed solitude and quiet study.

Not at all the kind of surroundings in which she would have expected to find the high-profile, socially-very-much-in-demand Nathan Bryce. But he had designed and built it for himself.

Confusion was tightening the band around Polly's

head. How many more facets were there to this complex man? Which was the *real* Nathan Bryce?

'I want you in bed,' he'd said. He was a powerful, virile man, and she had been left in no doubt as to the physical effect she had on him. She had given herself totally to the frighteningly wonderful feelings he aroused in her. Only now did it occur to her how easily he could have taken advantage of the situation.

Compared with his, her physical strength was laughable. Like one of the marauding buccaneers who used to terrorise the Mediterranean coasts, he could have taken her there and then, and she could have done little to stop him. But he hadn't.

Polly felt a strange tension deep inside her. She couldn't help thinking how different he was from Giles, who had never missed an opportunity to pressure her, using compliments and charm like velvet hammers in an effort to get him what he wanted.

Despite the turmoil within her a small ironic smile lifted the corners of her mouth. She'd never have to worry about Nathan Bryce trying to overwhelm her with charm. Ordinary civility was an uphill battle for him.

Laying one hand on the pale blue cotton lining of his sleeping-bag, she stroked it. Her eyes lost their focus and she sighed softly.

What would it be like to feel the weight of that lean, powerful body on hers, and lie skin to skin against him? What would it be like to explore and learn every inch of him with her fingertips, to touch and taste him and fill her lungs with the delicious musky scent that was uniquely his? What would it be like to fall asleep in the protecting shelter of his arms? What did he look like asleep? What would he look like in love?

Closing her eyes, she swallowed hard, shuddering

violently. Normally common sense and her instinct for self-protection, much sharpened since her disastrous relationship with Giles, would have outlawed such foolish thoughts before they even reached her conscious mind.

But this wasn't a normal situation. The adrenalin which had been pumping into her bloodstream since early the previous day had burned up all her reserves of energy.

Energy she had been unable to replace by eating because of her queasy stomach. Because of her weakened state her imagination had run riot. But it wouldn't happen again. It mustn't. She couldn't afford thoughts like those. Though tantalisingly seductive, they were fraught with peril.

Nathan Bryce might *want* her, but that was all. And it was not enough.

Straightening her legs out, she leaned forward to pull the zip halfway up the duvet-like sleeping-bag which, she realised belatedly, was actually two bags opened flat and zipped together.

Arranging the pillows against the padded head-rest, she slid down into the soft cocoon and, lying flat on her back, gazed up at the deckhead. She'd never be able to sleep, her mind was too active. Her thoughts whirled and tumbled like leaves in a gale.

But at least she was warm. Lovely and warm. Floating, drifting. . .

Nathan was talking to someone she couldn't see. His manner was very different from the one she was used to. He seemed quiet and thoughtful. He wasn't stern and scowling and barking orders.

Looking up, he caught sight of her. She tensed. But instead of the frowning anger she expected, his face lit up with pleasure. Leaving whoever it was he'd been talking to, he started towards her.

She felt as though she might burst with the joy that filled her. Lifting her arms, she held them out to him. He was close, so close: his lips warm, tender and cherishing as they moved on hers. It was a kiss like no other she had ever experienced. She had waited all her life for this moment.

She heard a sound and realised it came from her own throat. The gentle pressure on her lips suddenly wasn't there any more, and she felt bereft. Sadness overwhelmed her. She opened her eyes. And looked directly into Nathan's.

He slowly straightened to his full height and she realised he had been sitting on the bed leaning over her.

Fully awake now, Polly lay absolutely still, her mind racing as she tried to work out what was real and what had been part of her dream. Swallowing, she moistened her lips. His gaze flickered to her mouth. 'Did— did you just kiss me?' she croaked.

He nodded.

Polly scrambled up against the pillows, hugging the sleeping-bag to her chest. Sitting up in bed seemed somehow less intimate than lying down. 'You—you had no right——' she began. Why was it so hot? The cabin seemed airless.

His brows climbed. 'No *right*? Woman, you reached for me.'

'I did?' she gasped. 'No,' she shook her head quickly, 'you're making it up.' But as the vivid dream came back she realised he was telling the truth. Where had the dream ended and reality begun? 'I was asleep,' she finished. It was the truth, yet it sounded so lame.

'Do I take that as regret or apology?' he enquired.

Despite the lines of exhaustion bracketing his mouth and etched at the outer corners of his eyes, his gaze gleamed dangerously.

'Neither,' she retorted. 'I didn't know what was happening.'

'I expect Eve used the same excuse,' he commented drily.

Polly stared at him, uncomprehending. 'Eve?'

'The Garden of Eden?' he prompted.

She yanked the sleeping-bag even higher. 'Of course. Poor powerless Adam.' Her voice dripped sarcasm. 'The woman had tempted him. As if he'd had no choice in the matter.' She sniffed. 'Men have been blaming women ever since.'

Nathan shrugged. 'Can we help it if we're putty in your hands?'

Polly snorted in derision. 'Oh, come on. Who are you trying to kid? *You* are about as pliable as a lump of granite. And you've done nothing but snap and shout at me ever since we came on board.'

He tilted his head to one side, considering her. 'Yet still you hold out your arms to me with a smile that would melt an iceberg. Odd, that, wouldn't you say?'

Polly felt her entire body flush with heat. 'I——' *Was dreaming*, she was about to say, but stopped herself just in time. Heaven only knew what reaction *that* admission would provoke. 'I'd better get dressed. If you'll excuse me?' But her brave stab at cool politeness was mocked by her flushed cheeks and the way her sleep shirt was clinging to her sweat-dewed body.

'Of course.' His grave expression didn't match the ironic amusement in eyes which held darker shadows. 'I've brought you some tea.' He indicated the mug on top of the locker, then opened the cabin door. 'Make sure you put warm clothes on. It's much colder up there than it is in here.' His gaze held hers for a moment, then, turning abruptly, he went out.

As his footsteps receded down the passage, Polly's hand rose slowly to her mouth. She could still taste his kiss, still feel the firm yet gentle pressure of his lips. What did it mean?

Did it *mean* anything? Yes, it had, to her. But she was insane if she took it seriously. Nathan Bryce was a playboy, a womaniser. Of course his kisses were stirring. He'd had more than enough practice to become an expert.

Polly swallowed her tea. The hot liquid refreshed and strengthened her. Then she dressed quickly in jeans and a long-sleeved shirt and pulled on her thick Aran cardigan. How wrong she had been about not needing it.

As she left the cabin she took one of the oilskin jackets out the hanging locker. If she was prepared for the worst then, God willing, it wouldn't happen. Even if it didn't rain the jacket would help keep out the cold night wind.

Polly kept her head bent while Nathan helped her into her safety harness. She had been aware enough of him before. But now, with the memory of her dream and his kiss so vivid, it was ten times worse. She fought the urge to look at his mouth, terrified she would somehow betray herself.

'Remember,' he warned, tugging at the buckle to make sure it was securely fastened, 'you are not, in *any* circumstances, to take that off. And call me at once if there's the slightest change in the weather.' He made her repeat their course, then took a last look around. 'Right,' his haggard features were stern, 'she's all yours.' And God help you if you don't keep your wits about you and take care of her. He didn't actually say the words, but they were implicit in the final look he gave her before disappearing down the companionway.

Polly heard him moving about. After a while, through the partially open cabin hatch, she heard the bed creak beneath his weight. She visualised him drawing the sleeping-bag around him. The sound of a groan, swiftly followed by a muffled curse, made her jump. Then there was silence.

The sky was clear and studded with stars, The three-quarter moon lit a silver path across the inky water. As *Seawitch* creamed along with taut sails in the steady south-westerly breeze Polly's nervousness gave way to pride and pleasure.

Doggedly practising her seamanship to keep thoughts and images of Nathan at bay, she wasn't aware of time passing until she noticed that the sky ahead seemed lighter.

Gradually the greyness turned to pink. She watched, enthralled, as the sky blushed in an ever-widening arc. Deep rose merged with the turquoise and aquamarine of fast-fading night. The last few stars disappeared, extinguished by the splendour of the rising sun as shafts of golden light gilded the sea.

Polly was transfixed. The numbing cold which had crept up her legs from feet she could barely feel was forgotten. So was the ache in her hands as she clung to the wheel. 'Are you all right?' Nathan's tousled head appeared in the hatchway. He yawned.

She started violently. She hadn't heard him. 'I'm fine,' she replied automatically—then realised with a shock that she really was. Her nausea had gone and she was actually hungry.

He rubbed his face, his hand rasping over the heavy beard stubble.

'You look just like Gregory Peck in an old pirate movie.' Except that even with costume and make-up the star had looked less like a pirate than Nathan Bryce did at this moment. Polly grinned, delight at the glorious sunrise, and relief at feeling better adding warmth and brilliance to her smile.

Nathan gazed fixedly at her for a moment with an expression she couldn't fathom, then disappeared again. When he re-emerged a quarter of an hour later, wearing yesterday's denim shorts and white T-shirt topped by a guernsey with fraying cuffs, he had showered and shaved and his hair was freshly combed.

He was overpoweringly attractive. Polly looked quickly away. 'Did you sleep well?' she asked politely, keeping her eyes lowered as she unclipped her safety harness, stamping her feet to try and restore the circulation.

'No.' He scowled. 'Just put the kettle on, will you?'

'Definitely *not* a morning person,' she murmured. 'All right, I'm going.' She dived for the companionway as he swung round, glowering.

After freshening up, she hurried to the galley and made a big pot of coffee and a huge plateful of bacon sandwiches. Taking the tray up on deck, she offered him the plate, then helped herself and, mouth watering in anticipation, began to eat.

As she picked up her third sandwich she looked across at him, slightly self-conscious about her ravenous appetite. 'It's marvellous to actually want food again. I don't think I've ever enjoyed a meal so much. I can't believe how much better I feel.'

'Good,' came the terse reply. 'Take the wheel, will you? I'm going to get a forecast and lay a course for

Ibiza harbour. Then I have some phone calls to make.'
He didn't once look in her direction.

'Charming,' Polly muttered under her breath as he
vanished below. But she refused to allow his surliness
to burst her bubble of well-being. Some people simply
weren't at their best first thing in the morning.

When he came back on deck she tried once more to
make conversation. Without a word he leaned forward
and switched on the engine.

He had explained how important it was to recharge
the batteries. But choosing that particular moment to
do it was a rebuff as callous and shocking as a slap in
the face.

Stunned and bewildered, Polly stared at him. She
turned towards the companionway, then stopped.
Amazed at her own daring, she watched herself reach
out and flip off the ignition switch. The silence was
very loud.

'What the hell do you think you're doing?' Nathan
demanded.

Quaking inside, Polly stood her ground. 'It's not
easy to talk against the noise. And I want to know
what's wrong. Last night——' She wetted her lips,
fighting memories both seductive and painful. 'Last
night we managed to have a reasonable conversation.
Yet this morning you're rude, surly, and unapproach-
able. I think I've a right to know why.'

He gave her a blistering stare. 'You really have no
idea?'

'Look,' Polly tried desperately, 'I admit I was wrong
to let you believe I was an experienced sailor. At the
time,' she twined and untwined her fingers, 'there
didn't seem to be any choice. But I've worked really
hard to make up for it. I want to do my share, not be
a liability. Feeling so rotten certainly didn't help. But

that's passed off now. I've found my sea-legs. I'll be quicker and much more useful.' She ran out of breath. Her tentative smile brought no answering response. In fact, his features seemed to tighten into even harsher lines.

As she gazed at him in mute appeal he turned his back. Biting her lip, she drew herself up. 'OK.' She swallowed, steadying her voice. 'If this is the way you want it. It's your choice. But you can make the rest of the voyage by yourself. I'm getting off at Ibiza. Oh, don't worry,' her bitter hurt spilled over as he swung round, 'I'll see you get your money.'

'And how do you propose to do that?' he enquired. His tone was scathing and dismissive. But though he had masked it quickly she knew he was shaken by her announcement.

'I'll send a fax to my father.'

'Indeed?' His scepticism was plain. 'May I ask why you didn't do that in the first place?'

'No, you may not,' she said with a calmness that bore little resemblance to the chaos inside her. 'It's none of your business. But I'll tell you this,' she glared at him, her heart pounding, 'I'd rather work around the clock to get the money back to my father in time than spend one minute longer than I have to with a selfish, bad-tempered misery who was obviously born an expert at everything.'

Elation battled with fear as she watched various expressions chase across his face.

'What *are* you talking about?' he demanded at last.

Chin high, she met his narrowed gaze with undisguised hostility. 'Your rudeness, your infuriating superiority, and your lack of patience with anyone who isn't psychic enough to know what you want before you ask for it.' She held her breath. Let him get mad. She wasn't backing down. Someone should have said all this to him years ago. If he got angry, tough, she could always go below. She'd stay there until they docked in Ibiza if necessary.

He glowered at her. Then, to her startled amazement, his mouth twisted in a brief, shamefaced smile.

'It appears I owe you an apology.' He looked away and his shrug betrayed an uncharacteristic diffidence. 'These last two days haven't been easy for me.'

'They haven't been a barrel of laughs for me either,' Polly shot back. She took a breath, and tried to make her tone more conciliatory. 'I really have been trying my best——'

'I know,' he interrupted. 'Actually, you've done far better than I expected. I'm impressed.'

Polly stiffened. 'Then why have you been so rotten?' she cried.

His eyes glittered with a mixture of irony and astonishment. 'You really *don't* know?'

'I wouldn't be asking if I did,' she retorted. 'Is it business pressures? You do spend a lot of time on the radio telephone. Are there more problems with the meeting in Athens?' She hesitated as a thought occurred. 'Look, if it's anything to do with feeling some sort of responsibility towards me——'

'Polly,' he cut in drily, 'my feelings towards you are anything but responsible.' He glanced away for a moment, then his piercing gaze met and held hers. 'Do you have any idea of what is was like for me, trying to sleep in a bed still warm from your body and scented with that soap and powder you use?'

Her heart skipped a beat. She recalled his groan and the muffled curse that followed it. And as she remembered her own vivid imaginings a blush crept up her throat to flood her cheeks with hot colour. Her eyelashes fluttered down to hide feelings she dared not let him see. Not yet. Maybe not ever.

'Do you?' he demanded.

She looked up, bewildered. 'But you don't even like me.' Then suspicion clouded her face. 'Anyway, it's nothing new for you. You've shared a woman's bed before.'

'Not yours,' he said softly.

Polly flinched at the thrill that rippled through her. She wanted to tell him that he never would either, but her mind was awhirl with images of herself in Nathan's arms, on the soft padded cotton sleeping-bag, and she couldn't force the words out.

'I've never known anyone like you.' He sounded surprised. 'You make me very curious.'

She couldn't resist a sidelong glance at him. 'Oh? Why?'

'I have this problem with women. They tend to throw themselves at me.'

Polly eyes widened at this breathtaking conceit. She opened her mouth to make a suitably cutting retort, then closed it abruptly as she realised. Though he was deliberately sending himself up, he was also stating a simple fact.

Quite apart from all the pictures in the papers, she had seen it for herself at the presentation. The girls from the office had swarmed about him like bees around a honey jar, jockeying for position, anxious to be noticed.

Nathan's smile was slightly crooked. 'But you haven't. Why not? What's wrong with me?'

Polly swallowed the dryness in her throat. Thrilled to the core by his admission that she disturbed and aroused him, she was at the same time terrified. The wounds of the past were only just healing. Was Nathan

Bryce's interest in her genuine? Or simply a game to pass the time and add spice to the voyage?

'What's wrong with you?' she repeated, resting her forearms on the coach roof so she could hide her trembling hands. 'Apart from arrogance, bad temper, selfishness, and the manners of a dictator?' She shrugged. 'Absolutely nothing.'

Something flared in the depths of his gaze and his slow smile literally stopped her breath. Bending her head, she took a step towards the companionway.

'Where do you think you're going?' His voice was pleasant, but the undertone sent chills down her spine even as tiny flames licked her nerve-ends.

'I have things to do.' She reached for the empty plate and coffee-cups. 'Wash the dishes, make the bed——' She would willingly have bitten her tongue off. Even though they had occupied it separately, the fact that they had shared his bed created an intimacy that was impossible to ignore.

'Take the wheel,' Nathan ordered.

'But——'

'Take the wheel,' he repeated implacably, and stood aside, holding *Seawitch* on course with one hand. As Polly took his place he started down the companionway.

'Where are you going now?' she cried.

He seemed mildly surprised by the question. 'I've got to work out a new course.'

'What on earth for?' she demanded. 'You've just spent heaven knows how long checking our approach to Ibiza.'

He nodded. 'I know. But there's been a change of plan. We aren't going to Ibiza after all.'

Polly gaped at him. 'What? Why not?'

His smile was patient—*lethal*. 'It's very simple. You threatened to leave. I'm not ready to let you go.'

Her heartbeat thundered in her ears. 'But you can't——'

'Polly,' he shook his head, 'I'm a pirate, remember? I can do anything I want.'

Speechless, her heart racing, Polly clung to the wheel. Already her sailing ability had reached a level where she was able to make the minor corrections to hold the boat on course without even thinking.

'You can't force me——'

'I'll never force you to do anything against your will.'

'You won't let me get off,' she countered.

'That's different.' Nathan frowned at her. 'Have you forgotten? When I paid your bail you were released into *my* custody. If you leave the boat, except in my company or with my express permission, you'll be breaking the law. Besides, we made a deal in Gibraltar. It's not negotiable.' The cold note of finality in his voice warned her not to pursue the matter.

'What about fresh water? And food? And fuel?' she demanded, clutching at straws. His admission that his distance and antipathy had, in reality, been a vain attempt to fight his attraction to her had totally unnerved her. She was being drawn into ever more dangerous waters by the profound attraction she felt towards him.

'We have enough,' he replied calmly. 'Switch the engine on to charge.' He turned towards the companionway.

Polly's grip on the wheel tightened as, head and heart in raging conflict, she sought wildly for some means of escape. Was that smudge off to the left the island of Ibiza? Once he went below, if she turned the boat in that direction, just a few degrees at a time, would he notice?

'Don't even think about it,' Nathan warned.

She started, her indrawn breath a soft hiss. She hadn't realised he was still there, still watching her. Turning her head away, she closed her eyes. How had he known?

'Who are you running from, Polly?' he asked quietly. 'Me? Or yourself?' Without waiting for an answer he disappeared down the ladder.

CHAPTER EIGHT

'Shouting at me isn't a lot of help,' Polly blazed, flinging pencil and ruler down on the chart spread over the tray balanced on her knee, then lifting her head to glare at him.

Nathan straightened up. Holding *Seawitch* on course with one hand, he pushed the other through hair already rumpled by previous displays of frustration. 'Well, how many more times do I have to explain it?' he roared.

'As many as it takes for me to understand,' Polly shouted back. 'Going all autocractic and impatient won't drum it in any quicker.' The warm breeze did nothing to cool her flushed cheeks. 'You might be a brilliant designer, Nathan, and I'm sure you know everything there is to know about sailing. But you're a lousy teacher!'

His features hardened into an expressionless mask, but not before she had glimpsed an instant's pure shock.

'Would you care to elaborate?' he gritted.

Polly felt her stomach nerves flutter uneasily, but she had come too far and put up with too much to back down now. 'To be a successful teacher it's not enough simply to *know*. You have to have the ability to put that knowledge across.'

'Are you saying I don't?' he enquired in a dangerously soft voice that slid down her spine like melting ice.

But she wasn't going to let him browbeat her. He

was far too used to people backing down and deferring to him. She gave a careless shrug. 'No one's brilliant at everything.' That was as far as she was going towards conciliation.

His eyes glittered fiercely. 'Of course, it does help if the student has more than one brain cell.'

'Now isn't that just typical?' Polly's mouth curled. 'Blaming me for your own inadequacy.'

They glowered at one another for several seconds. Then she braced herself, heaving a deep sigh. 'Right,' she said wearily, 'let's go through it again.'

'We'll have some coffee first,' Nathan decided. But as Polly automatically started to put the chart aside he gestured to her to remain where she was. 'No, I'll get it. You take the wheel for a spell.' He disappeared down the ladder.

This had been the pattern of the past two days. Polly recognised Nathan's insistence on her learning how to navigate as an attempt to keep the lid on a situation which was escalating rapidly out of control.

Relieved yet disappointed, and furious at her own inconsistency, Polly jumped at the chance to learn a new skill. She was desperate to keep her mind fully occupied. She wanted to be so busy she wouldn't have either time or energy to wonder about him, to dream, or hope.

Of course, it didn't turn out like that. Working so closely together made her more aware of him, not less. But, despite the electric atmosphere, they were beginning to function as a team. She was keen to learn, and his trust in her had grown to the point where they alternated the night watches so both had the opportunity for more rest.

Not that she was sleeping all that well. Nor, from the sounds of tossing and turning that drifted up through the deck hatch in the quiet dark hours of her watch, was Nathan. But neither spoke of it.

He had made no attempt to kiss her again—in fact, he seemed deliberately to avoid getting too close to her at all. But occasionally, when her guard slipped and she allowed her eyes to meet his, she saw in his gaze the mingled hostility and desire which reflected all too accurately her own conflicting emotions

Even when one of them was on deck and the other below there was no escape. They were still prisoners of the attraction which, under the guise of antipathy, had arced between them the moment Nathan had entered the Customs office.

Balanced lightly on the balls of her feet, Polly turned the wheel a few degrees as *Seawitch* heeled over. Wearing her navy shorts and a jade-green polo shirt, she felt cool and fresh. Wind and sun had gilded her arms and legs honey-brown, hiding the last of the fading bruises. She felt physically fitter and more alive than she could ever remember. Only the violet shadows beneath her eyes, so out of place in her tanned and glowing face, hinted at the emotional upheaval she was enduring.

Thin streaks of high cloud trailed across an azure sky. A fresh breeze curled the tops of the waves into tiny frills of foam that glistened white on the sapphire sea.

Polly licked her lips. They tasted salty from the fine spray *Seawitch* threw into the hazy air as she dug her elegant nose into the waves before tossing them aside.

Nathan emerged from the companionway with two mugs of coffee. He passed one to Polly but, instead of taking over the helm again, seated himself in *her* usual corner of the cockpit, stretching his long legs out and crossing his ankles.

Swallowing a mouthful of coffee, she forced herself not to look at him. 'Shall I bring my mattress and sleeping-bag up in a minute? They're still not dry.'

Nathan squinted up at the masthead, then gazed into his coffee-mug. 'No. There's not enough room with both of us up here. And with all the spray flying around they'd get even wetter.'

'But surely with this breeze,' she started, 'and the sun's really hot. . .'

'No.' It was cold and final.

'OK.' Turning her head, Polly sipped her coffee and gazed out over the expanse of water. 'But we can't count on this weather lasting. And this is the second day you've refused to let me bring my bedding up. It'll never dry at this rate.'

He glared at her, his features taut. 'Polly, the last thing I want right now is an argument about beds.'

She flushed. 'It's just—well, I'd have thought you'd be glad to have your cabin to yourself.'

'What's the matter? Aren't you comfortable?' he demanded, his voice harsh.

'Of course I am. It's not that.' The bed was wonderfully comfortable, the pillows soft, and the sleeping-bags light but warm as toast. In fact, it was far more welcoming than the bed in her flat. 'But——'

'Yes?'

'Nothing. It doesn't matter.' She looked away, closing her eyes and lifting her face to the breeze.

'No, tell me. I insist.'

She swivelled round, bristling at his tone.

His mouth twisted in a brief grin of self-mocking apology. 'Please?'

Polly shrugged. She had to swallow before she could reply. 'I'm—I'm not used to sharing, that's all.'

Nathan's laugh was short and hard. '*Sharing*? We're never even in the damned cabin at the same time.'

That was true. Since the night he kissed her he had woken her for her watch by hammering on the deck-head until she shouted that she was on her way. And he was always up before it was time for her to call him.

'You know what I mean.' Polly's voice was anguished. Sliding into the warmth he had just left, inhaling the scent of him on the pillows, surrounded by his clothes, books and possessions, she could feel her resolve to keep him at arm's length ebbing relent-lessly away.

She kept reminding herself of the stories about him in the gossip columns, of his reputation as a woman-iser. But working with him each day, learning from him, trying to hide her glowing pleasure when grudging approval replaced irritation and impatience in his piercing gaze, the warnings grew fainter and fainter.

'C—could you take the wheel?' she asked. 'I—I just want to go below for a moment.'

Silently he drained his mug and, rising to his feet, handed it to her. As she turned away he gently caught the nape of her neck with his free hand.

His touch lanced through her like a lightning bolt, clenching every muscle and tightening every nerve before filling her with liquid heat.

'Don't go,' he said softly. 'Stay and talk to me.'

She didn't look round. She didn't dare. 'I'll be back in a minute,' she managed.

He took his hand away, but as she stumbled down the ladder she could still feel its warm weight.

In the shower-room she rinsed her face with cold water. As she dried, she caught sight of herself in the mirror. She lowered the towel slowly. Haunted eyes stared back at her. What was she to do? If only she could get right away from him for a while, then she'd be able to cope. She'd get all these wild ridiculous yearnings under control. She'd be able to view the whole episode in perspective: see it for what it was, a brief flirtation brought about by proximity, boredom, and lack of alternative company.

Misery darkened her gaze. She had to face facts. She was already in way over her head. Nathan Bryce had woken in her feelings she hadn't known existed.

She had thought she was in love with Giles, but he had never aroused this heady excitement in her, or made her skin tingle when he came anywhere near. He had never caused her breath to catch in her throat or her mouth to dry with a mixture of hope and dread that he might reach for her.

When they first met, Giles had made her feel special, cherished and cared for. But because she had not felt ready to go to bed with him he had punished her by trying to destroy her self-confidence. And he had very nearly succeeded.

With Nathan it had all happened the other way around. In spite of their mutual dislike and hostility, he had helped her discover abilities and a depth of feeling she hadn't dreamed she possessed.

Never before had she argued so passionately with a man, hating him and wanting him with an intensity that frightened her. She was exhausted yet filled with so much energy she couldn't keep still.

'Nathan,' she whispered. Closing her eyes briefly, she bent her head, clutching the basin with both hands. Drawing a deep breath, she straightened her spine. Wanting what you couldn't have was a waste of time. Nathan Bryce was attracted to her, but that was all. She had to accept that. Just as she had to accept that, for her, it would never be enough.

Swallowing the stiffness in her throat, she folded the towel neatly on to the rail and combed her hair. Then, with a final glance in the mirror, reassured that she had her wayward emotions once more under control, she left her tiny sanctuary.

As she stepped out on to the deck, Nathan gave her a brief smile. At the corners of his mouth and around his eyes Polly saw echoes of her own strain. Banishing the tug of sympathy, she looked away quickly.

'We'll make land in a few hours,' he told her.

She gazed at him in surprise. 'How? Where?' Since steering clear of Ibiza, he had refused to tell her where their next port of call would be.

He pointed ahead through the haze to a darker smudge on the horizon. 'That's Sicily.'

Standing close alongside him following the direction of his outstretched arm, Polly felt the skin all down her left side prickling as if static electricity was leaping between them.

'We'll land at Marsala, a sea- and fishing-port on the south-western coast. It's renowned for its wine. Of course,' he added drily, 'that wouldn't interest you at all. But the markets have wonderful fruit and vegetables and an amazing variety of fresh fish.'

She moistened her lips. 'And we're actually going ashore? Both of us?'

Nathan glanced at her. 'It wouldn't be wise to try and run away.' His eyes were cold blue steel. 'There's nowhere you could go that I wouldn't find you.' Tightening the mainsail, he continued pleasantly, 'Just behind the old port there's a restaurant that serves swordfish steaks with a herb and lemon dressing that's out of this world. We'll eat there tonight. It'll save you having to cook. Not that I've any complaints on that score,' he added. 'I've never eaten as well as I have on this trip.'

'There's no need to sound quite so surprised,' Polly sniffed, her heart still beating fast. *'There's nowhere you could go that I wouldn't find you'*. 'I told you I could cook.'

'You also told me—*allowed me to believe*—that you could sail,' he responded immediately.

'I'm learning,' she shot back. 'And I bet I've absorbed more about seamanship than you would have about cooking.'

'Which presumably makes me the better teacher,' he returned with a dryness that made her want to pummel him with her fists from sheer frustration. 'Tell me something,' he demanded before she could speak. 'Why don't you have a permanent job? You're brainy——'

Polly's eyebrows shot up. 'What? With only one functioning grey cell?'

He silenced her with a look. 'As I was saying before I was so rudely interrupted, you're intelligent as well as beautiful. You could have built a substantial career.'

'I wasn't sure what I wanted to do. Which made me the family oddity.'

She sat down in her usual corner. She needed distance between them as she fought to smother a treacherous joy that he should think her beautiful. She had never considered herself so. Yet his manner made it clear that he was simply stating a fact, not flattering with a compliment. And that made it all the more thrilling, especially when she recalled some of the women he'd been photographed with.

'Explain.' Nathan's tone was a blend of command and encouragement.

Polly shrugged. 'Both my parents are high achievers,

And my two sisters had their futures planned by the time they were ten. Louise is a GP and Sarah is a brilliant pianist. My parents are terribly proud of them. Mother's cup really overflowed last year when Louise had her third child and Sarah married a famous conductor.'

The sardonic grin that twisted Nathan's mouth was tempered by the unexpected sympathy in his eyes. 'Obviously you attended the wedding.'

Startled by his understanding, Polly nodded and pulled a wry face. 'It bore a fair resemblance to the Spanish Inquisition. All the relations fired the same questions at me. It was almost funny. When was I going to get a *proper* job, and if I didn't, or couldn't, when was I going to get married and settle down.'

Nathan's expression was unreadable. 'What did you say?'

'What I believe. That getting married and having children shouldn't be something you do because your family thinks it's a good idea, or because you're not much good at anything else.'

'Why not? It's the ultimate aim for most women.'

'How would you know?' Polly was derisive.

'Come on!' His tone matched hers. 'I'm thirty-six years old. I'm single. And I have a job which keeps me in the public eye. I'm a prime target.'

Images of the girls in the office, the flutter of female interest and appreciation at the presentaion, and the response of the woman in the ladies' room at the restaurant in Gibraltar flashed across Polly's mind.

'No one's caught you get, though,' she pointed out, her throat oddly dry.

'True.' His smile had a bitter edge. 'The kind of childhood I had tends to make you wary of trusting people. Besides, it's not *me* they want, it's the glamorous, high-profile media image. What's your excuse?'

'For what?'

'Avoiding marriage.'

She shot him a look of exasperation. 'I haven't exactly been overwhelmed with proposals,' she retorted, 'not of marriage, anyway. But in any case, I felt I needed to know who *I* was first.'

'And do you?'

'Know myself?' Polly's crooked smile masked a stab of painful yearning. 'I've learned more than I expected,' she admitted. Or was prepared for.

He looked hard at her for a moment, and she tensed. But he didn't press for an explanation. 'So what are the benefits of being a temporary secretary?'

'Apart from earning very good money, I find the work interesting and a challenge.'

'You enjoy the constant change and variety?' His glance was brief and enigmatic.

'Yes,' she nodded. They were talking about her job, she reminded herself. Nothing else, just her job. So why was she beginning to feel nervous?

'What about children?'

She blinked, thrown by the sudden change of subject. 'What about them?'

'Don't you want some of your own?'

'I haven't thought about it,' she lied, shielding her eyes with one hand as she tilted her head back to look at clouds like cotton wool balls racing overhead.

The previous night she had dreamed she was sitting up in Nathan's bunk, holding a baby to her breast. As the tiny head, covered in silky black hair, nestled warmly in the palm of her hand, she had looked up and met eyes full of tenderness and love, eyes the colour of slate. Nathan Bryce's eyes.

She had woken then, jerking bolt upright, her heart pounding against her ribs. The cabin had been in darkness, and she had been alone.

Head bent, overwhelmed by a grief she didn't understand, she had clenched the cover in her fists, hating him with every ounce of strength she possessed. There was no escape, no defence against him, even in her sleep.

Eventually she had slid wearily down beneath the cover and drifted off again. Having forced her to recognise the truth of her feelings, her unconscious had left her alone. There had been no more dreams.

'Does that mean you don't want any?' Nathan persisted.

She started, jolted out of her reverie. 'I never said that——'

'But your lifestyle keeps you constantly on the move,' he pointed out. 'How will you ever meet a prospective father for your children if you're never in one place for more than a week or two?' A new note entered his voice. 'Or is that the whole point of being only "temporary"?'

Polly frowned, suddenly wary. 'What do you mean?'

His gaze flickered over her. 'Well,' he drawled, 'you have to admit it's the perfect camouflage for someone who's not mature enough to handle the commitment of a long-term relationship.'

She flinched, then immediately went on to the attack. 'You're a fine one to talk. With your track record I don't know how you have the nerve to lecture *me* on commitment.'

'Men and women are different——' he began impatiently.

'How observant,' Polly cut in. 'I had already noticed that myself.'

'I was referring to the way men view relationships.'

She hugged her arms across her chest in an unconscious gesture of self-protection. 'The majority of men don't want a relationship. They simply want sex.'

He shook his head. 'You're too sweeping in your judgement. Not all men are like that.'

'Oh, really?' Polly's irony couldn't smother the pain that lanced through her. She turned her head away, afraid it might show on her face.

All Giles had wanted in return for the small gifts he showered on her was affection. But she had quickly learned that his definition of the word went far beyond what she understood it to mean. The gifts had become a pressure, an embarrassment, and her refusal to accept them had made him manipulative. Soon he had begun to convince her that there was something wrong with her, that she wasn't normal.

His change of tactics had been so cunningly disguised that she hadn't realised what was happening. Then one day the mask had slipped, and beneath the apparent loving concern she had glimpsed spite and sadism.

The row that followed had left her deeply shaken, as much at her own blindness to the kind of man he really was as by the dreadful things he had said.

Was she on the verge of falling into the same trap again? 'Then perhaps I've just been unlucky with the ones I've met.'

'My point exactly.' His eyes glittered. 'If you're continually on the move, what time or opportunity is there for interaction at any but the most superficial level?'

'Well, if that's all that's on offer,' Polly retorted, 'I'll pass, thanks all the same. I *like* my job.' Even as she said it she recalled the growing doubts and disgust which had been another spur driving her to accept Clive's invitation. But how could she admit to them after all she'd said?

'Of course you like it,' he mocked. 'You like it so much you agreed to sail across the Mediterranean, with a man you'd only met a couple of times, regardless of the fact that you didn't know one end of a boat from the other.' He shook his head. 'If I didn't know just how much you like your job I might actually think you were looking for an escape from it.'

Polly hugged her legs tighter. 'All right,' she admitted. 'But it wasn't work I wanted to get away from, just the kind of people I sometimes have to work *for*. Men who can't keep their minds on their job, or their hands to themselves.'

His expression hardened, became a mask that hid whatever he was thinking. 'You can't altogether blame them. You are extremely attractive.'

'And that gives them the right to try and maul me?' she flared, unable to contain her hurt and anger.

'No,' he said softly. 'Of course it doesn't. To look is one thing—that's everyone's right. But to touch. . .' As he turned his head away she saw a muscle jumping at the point of his jaw.

The air between them was suddenly charged. Polly stood up. 'I—I'll go and——' Her voice faltered as she dived for the ladder. She hadn't the faintest idea what she was going below to do. All she knew was that she had to get away from him before she betrayed herself.

'Polly?' His voice had the roughness of sandpaper. 'Look at me.'

All the old arrogance was there, the dictatorial note of command. But beneath it she heard something else. It was that which struck an answering chord within her and made her stop. Slowly, unable to help herself, she turned, raising her head to meet his gaze.

'I want to touch. No,' the brief self-mocking laugh seemed to tear at this throat, 'I want far more than that. I want to know you the way no man has ever known a woman before.'

'How *can* you?' Polly burst out. 'You don't believe me. You don't trust me.'

'You're wrong,' he grated. 'I've learned a lot about you in the past few days. Far more than I expected, and more than you realise. I know now that you couldn't have been involved in Clive Kemp's drug-running plans. And as for trusting you. . .' His gaze swept the length of the boat. '*Seawitch* is worth a great deal of money, but, if anything happened to her, I could always build another yacht. I only have one life. . .and while I slept it was in your hands. Isn't that trust?'

His eyes darkened. 'I want you more than I've ever wanted anything in my life. But I gave you my word— nothing against your will.' His gaze held hers. 'Would it be against your will, Polly? Would it?'

She was trapped, as helpless as if she'd been bound in chains. She longed to give in to the desire in his eyes and her own body's urging. But without love, passion was just a bubble. And when it burst there was nothing left. Yet how could she think of *love* in connection with this ruthless, powerful man? They had only met a few days ago. All right, so there was far more depth to Nathan than his media image suggested. But what did he really want? Was it just the thrill of the chase? Would the moment of conquest signal the end of his interest in her?

In all her postings she had never met a man like him. There *was* no one else like him. He was his own unique, contradictory self. And she was falling in love with him.

He would complete her transition from girl to woman. But at what cost? For it would not be just her body he took possession of, but her heart and soul as well.

'P—please.' Her voice cracked. 'Don't—I——' Her eyes filled.

'It's all right,' he said softly. 'I'll wait. It's your decision, Polly.'

'Do you think that makes it easier?' she cried, angrily brushing away the tears.

His crooked smile blended gentleness and irony. 'What else can I say?' His features tightened. 'Don't make me wait too long, that's all.'

Polly felt small and slight beside him, but her chin rose defiantly. 'Is that a threat?'

Snaking out one strong brown hand, Nathan caught the nape of her neck and hauled her towards him.

Gasping at the totally unexpected movement, and the searing shock of his touch, Polly stared up into eyes that gleamed with cold fire.

'No, sweetheart,' he growled. 'Just a warning. I'm a man, Polly, flesh and blood. I'm not short on self-control, but. . .' He let the sentence trail off into a silence that vibrated. Then he bent his head and his mouth claimed hers.

As her eyes closed she heard her own swift intake of breath. The tip of his tongue flicked, hot and silky, over her lower lip and gently explored the soft inner flesh.

She felt as if she was falling and her hand came up to steady herself. Beneath the roughness of the woollen guernsey she could feel the steady thud of his heartbeat. Warmed by his body heat, her fingers spread out against his chest as if to absorb him.

He drew her closer and, helpless against a tide of subtle, exquisite sensation that made her head swim, she relaxed against him, boneless and pliant. His hold tightened, his kiss growing deeper, more demanding. His fingers encircled the top of her spine and his muscular forearm held her clamped to the upper half of his body as he plundered her mouth.

Hardly aware of what she was doing, Polly slid her hand up to his shoulder. The muscles were iron-hard beneath his sweater. Her fingers strayed lightly over the back of his neck and into his thick curling hair. Her other arm crept around his waist. This was a million times better than dreams. This was real.

And suddenly she was afraid. She would be hurt again. She fought her fear. This was different. Nathan was different. She tried to hold on to the heady rapture that was sweeping her along like a river in flood. But as it receded, and she became increasingly aware of the strength of Nathan's desire for her, the urgent hunger in his kisses, her fear became overwhelming. She froze, then tried to push him away. 'No!' The word was a muffled, ragged cry.

Immediately Nathan lifted his head, tearing his lips from hers. Cloudy and unfocused for a moment, his eyes quickly regained their normal piercing clarity. But his face was drawn, the bronzed skin tight and flushed across his cheekbones as he struggled to control the powerful emotions that gripped him.

Startled by the swiftness with which he had released her, Polly moistened lips that felt swollen, but the words wouldn't come. Helpless, she gazed up at him. Her mind was a tangled confusion of fear, regret, apology, and a treacherous yearning still to be held fast against him.

'Th—thank you,' she stuttered as she stumbled backwards, her teeth chattering. Reaction to the violence of her own feelings had left her shivery. She was on the verge of tears, relieved yet unbelievably desolate.

She saw what his control was costing him. She bent her head in a quick, brief nod.

'Why don't you go and have a shower and decide what you're going to wear for our dinner date tonight?' Though it was phrased as a suggestion, Nathan's rasping tone made the words an order.

Recognising his need to be alone which, she acknowledged, was probably even greater than hers, Polly gave a quick nod and went below.

As she rummaged in her locker for her one suitable garment, a calf-length, multicoloured crinkle cotton skirt, the first tremors of anticipation started in her stomach. She was looking forward to standing on dry land once more. And to the possibility of seeing something of the Sicilian town. The prospect of eating a meal that someone else had prepared and cooked and would be clearing away was also very pleasant.

But the uneasy excitement that smouldered deep within her, like a banked-down fire waiting to be stirred into leaping life, was for what might come after.

Nathan's persistent questioning indicated a desire to know more about her. He had used subtlety and goading to make her reveal more than she intended. He had left her in no doubt that he wanted to take her to bed. And she had been startled by the strength and abandon of her own response.

But the word love had not been mentioned. Despite his apparent interest he had given her no clue as to

whether his future plans might include her. He had
made no commitment, given no promise. There was
just her and him and this voyage: a capsule of time
separate from their normal lives. The decision was
hers: *what was she going to do?*

CHAPTER NINE

THE golden sunlight of late afternoon gilded the shabby waterfront buildings. Behind the town scrub-covered hills were backed by hazy distant mountains. But between town and hills Polly could see neat vineyards, groves of olive and citrus trees, and the strips and oblongs of intensive vegetable cultivation.

Passing the old port, where the weather-worn fishing fleet was moored in tidy rows against the quay, they headed under power into Porta Nuova. Keeping clear of the wharves where machinery roared and clanked as cargoes were being discharged from or loaded on to rust-streaked ships with flaking paint, Nathan tied *Seawitch* to the rickety wooden pontoon reserved for yachts in transit.

'I'm going to the harbourmaster's office to get this lot dealt with,' he raised a sheaf of forms and permits, 'then I'll refill the fuel and water tanks. If you want to save yourself some time with the washing there's a launderette just along there.' He pointed to a street leading off the main quay. 'I've left my stuff wrapped in a towel on the bed. Got your list?' He barely gave Polly time to nod. 'You're sure you can manage on your own?'

'Of course,' she replied with far more confidence than she actually felt. But there was so much to do, and it would take twice as long if Nathan had to do it all himself. Besides, she needed to keep busy. The last thing she wanted right now was time to think. For her thoughts just went round in agonising circles.

When she returned two hours later, pausing to unhitch her skirt, which had caught on the wire safety railing, she could hear Nathan cursing angrily.

'It must have taken a lot of practice to become so fluent,' she called down the hatch to let him know she was back. She turned to descend the ladder.

'It goes with the territory when you work with boats,' he snarled, and muttered something violent under his breath.

Halfway down she stopped, leaned against the rungs, and heaved the bulging net bags over the coaming. 'Nathan,' she said over her shoulder, 'I don't know if it's important——'

'Here,' he interrupted brusquely, 'let me.' Coming to her side, he reached up, took the heavy bags as though they were weightless, and dumped them on the galley worktop.

'Thanks.' Polly let her breath out in a whoosh of relief, looking down to check how far she still had to go. 'I'm sure my arms are at least two inches longer than when I set out.'

Stepping off the last rung, she turned. She hadn't expected him to be simply standing there, watching her, and her breath caught in a small gasp as she almost collided with him.

During her absence Nathan had showered and changed into fawn trousers and a pale blue polo shirt. His thick hair, still damp and scored with comb marks, was springing back into its usual lustrous waves. He had shaved too, and the crisp scent of cologne mingled with the fresh fragrance of the soap he had used.

He filled her senses. And when the nerve-ends in her skin detected his body warmth across the short distance that separated them, her whole body responded, vibrating like a violin string. The magnetic pull was overpowering.

Involuntarily, she swayed forward. She saw his hands curl into white-knuckled fists and knew he was fighting to keep them at his sides.

She turned away quickly. This was no game. Playing with fire would get her burned. And though she longed to lose herself in the flames, to be consumed and reborn, she was also terribly afraid. Not so much of what would happen. She knew vaguely what to expect. And intuition told her that with Nathan it would be very different from the painful, greedy, and self-absorbed fumbling Giles had inflicted on her before she had succeeded in fighting him off.

What she dreaded was the prospect of facing life without Nathan once he had made her his. He might be able simply to take love where he found it, enjoy the moment and then move on. For her it could never be like that.

She had watched girl friends drift from affair to affair which always began with such certainty that 'this time it will be different', and inevitably ended in tears with the realisation that it wasn't.

Polly had recognised then that men could not value a woman who didn't value herself. It had nothing to do with teasing or playing hard to get. What it really came down to was self-respect. And she had never known a man she felt was worthy of the greatest gift she had to offer: herself, body and soul. But that was before she had met Nathan Bryce, when this complex, attractive, abrasive man was still simply a name and a photograph in a gossip column.

How cruelly ironic it was that the first man to capture her heart and awaken her senses, the man she had waited and longed for, should be metaphorically a ship passing in the night. Could the ecstasy of loving him outweigh the agony of losing him?

Careful to avoid his glittering gaze, she edged past into the galley and began unpacking. 'I presume you had a reason for that very colourful outburst?' she said lightly, far too busy to look up. 'What's the problem?'

'Several spring to mind,' he growled in a tone loaded with meaning. 'But at that particular moment I was cursing the VHF set. The blasted thing's on the blink again. It started playing up yesterday.' He glowered at the offending piece of equipment. 'I've phoned the agent in Palermo, but he can't get a replacement set sent down before tomorrow afternoon.' He frowned. 'I don't suppose one extra day here would put us that far behind. We've made pretty good time up to now.'

'Not stopping at Ibiza must have helped,' Polly said drily.

The lift of one dark brow told her he recognised the gibe. Turning his back on the receiver, he folded his arms and leaned against the chart table. 'So, what did you think of the market?'

Relieved that he had decided not to respond to her deliberately provocative remark, Polly was, at the same time, irritated. All right, so maybe she was being unreasonable. But it just seemed that he held all the cards, he made all the decisions. That wasn't true either.

She made a wry face. 'It was. . .loud.' After the relative peacefulness of the boat the market's noise, colour, and tantalising mixture of smells had made her senses reel.

Shallow wooden boxes piled high with green and red peppers, plump tomatoes, cucumbers, courgettes, new potatoes, and shiny purple aubergines, were laid out on tables and in rows on the ground. There were baskets of almonds and fresh apricots, trays of red and yellow plums, lemons and oranges. One long trestle-table spread with clean cloths and protected from the sun by a crude canopy was laden with cheeses of every shape, size and consistency. Another held an array of cured meats, hams, spicy sausages and salamis.

Her only problem had been one of choice. After buying fresh bread she had gone on to the fish market where boxes full of melting ice displayed what was left of the morning's catch, much of which she didn't recognise.

'I just wandered around and watched for a few minutes, to see how things were done,' she said over her shoulder, stowing a small block of fresh Parmesan in an airtight container before putting it in the fridge. She giggled. 'I've never seen such a performance. The customers complain about price, quality, and even colour, for all I know. The traders argue and plead. And it's all done with flashing eyes, waving arms, tossed heads and wringing hands. Eventually the women pick out what they want, the traders praise their keen eyes and good sense—at least, I assume that's what they're praising. Money changes hands and everyone is delighted.'

'You've had yourself quite a time,' Nathan observed. His mouth curved in amusement, but his narrowed gaze was thoughtful, as though her observations had surprised him.

Polly sighed. 'Haggling definitely loses something in sign language. But yes, it was fun.'

Her own smile faded as she closed a cupboard door. 'It was odd, though. The woman in charge of the launderette was quite different. It wasn't her clothes. She wore the usual black dress, and a black scarf around her hair. I don't suppose she was more than forty, yet—— It wasn't that she looked old, but there was something about her, as if she was somehow apart from what was going on.'

She recalled her own efforts, with few words and much gesturing, to find out if she could collect the washing, all clean and dried, in two hours. The woman had watched distantly, then inclined her head in dignified assent.

'Grief has that effect sometimes,' Nathan said quietly. 'If we were to stay longer you'd see many like her. Sicily is still trapped in its own past. Perhaps because it's an island old customs die hard here. Family feuds last for generations, and slurs on honour are avenged by murder.'

Polly's bright cotton skirt and sleeveless white broderie anglaise top had been perfect for shopping in the balmy warmth. But the images of violence and tragedy evoked by Nathan's words chilled her, and gooseflesh pimpled her arms.

He looked round. 'Did you pick it up?' he asked.

Still thinking about the woman and her aura of sadness, Polly started. 'Did I pick what up?'

'The washing.'

'No, I didn't,' she replied tartly. 'I've only got two hands, and though you were probably too busy kicking the VHF set to notice, I was already loaded like a packhorse. Oh, that reminds me——'

'I'll get it,' Nathan cut in, glancing at his watch. 'I won't be long.' He moved forward to the ladder. 'As soon as I get back we'll go and eat. Tell me then.' He hesitated, then vanished through the hatchway.

Polly stared after him, then, with a shrug, went into the tiny shower-room. She was probably making something out of nothing. No doubt when she told Nathan he would simply say, 'So what?' But what she had seen had certainly given her a shock.

She rinsed her hands and face, and combed her windblown curls into a smooth feathery cap. The fresh air and exercise had given her skin a radiant bloom that didn't need enhancement.

There was no disguising the strain around her eyes, or the plum-coloured shadows beneath them. But lack of sleep due to the four-hour night watches was a perfectly reasonable, if not wholly true, explanation for both.

With hands that weren't quite steady Polly took the top off her lipstick. The soft shade of coral was the perfect finishing touch.

She thought of the woman in the launderette and shivered. Was it really better to love and lose than to try and avoid the inevitable pain by not loving at all?

She heard Nathan's footsteps on the pontoon. With a final searching look at the haunted image in the mirror she drew herself up with a deep breath and walked down the narrow passage to meet him.

They were the only customers in the restaurant. 'It's too early in the season for tourists, and too early in the day for the locals,' Nathan explained. 'The Mediterranean peoples rarely sit down to dinner much before nine.'

The view from their table by the window took Polly's breath away. The sun, a huge ball of fire low on the horizon, had turned the sea pewter-grey and edged the streaks of peach and rose-hued cloud with molten silver.

While they ate their first course, a delicately flavoured clear soup, Nathan told her about the winemaking establishments which lay along the shore to the south of the town.

'An Englishman named Woodhouse introduced winemaking to the town in 1773, and his fir... is still operating from the same premises. W~~ ... you like a bottle to take back with you?'

Polly started to shake her head, but he didn't give her the chance to say anything.

'How stupid of me. You don't drink. Besides,' his face was set and hard, 'I don't suppose this trip is something you'll particularly want to remember.'

Polly opened her mouth, then looked quickly away before she betrayed her anguish. How could she tell him that every moment they had spent together was engraved on her soul? That she could never forget even if she wanted to? That her entire outlook on life had been turned upside-down?

She heard the clink of the dishes being taken away, then, from the corner of her eye, glimpsed movement as Nathan leaned forward.

'Why wouldn't you ask your father to put up bail for you?' His lowered voice was harsh. His gaze pierced her soul.

His generosity had got her out of gaol, and she had misled him about her sailing ability. He was entitled to the truth.

'I didn't want them to know,' she said quietly. 'Not unless it was absolutely unavoidable.' She raised her eyes to meet his. 'My mother's quite convinced that what she calls my "footloose lifestyle" is a recipe for disaster. But all I wanted was a bit of independence, a chance to find myself and discover what I really wanted from life.'

Nathan's eyes drilled into hers. 'And do you know yet?'

Yes. I want this voyage to last forever. She swallowed, but was saved from having to answer by the arrival of their swordfish steaks, brought in person by the restaurant owner who, Nathan had told her, was also the cook.

Polly's relief at the interruption must have made her smile of thanks warmer than she realised, for the lumbering bear of a man, swathed in a spotless white apron from his ripple of stubbled chins to the turn-ups of his elephantine trousers, beamed back. And after putting her plate in front of her he kissed the bunched tips of his pudgy fingers and shot rolling-eyed glances of admiration at her as he murmured to Nathan.

Polly felt a blush warm her cheeks and looked down at the food. In spite of the tension between her and Nathan the aromatic scent of the cooked fish in its herb and lemon dressing made her mouth water.

'Would you like me to tell you what he said?' Nathan enquired gravely as their host hurried back to the kitchen.

'No, thank you,' she replied quickly.

'It's quite repeatable,' Nathan assured her. 'Paolo recognises a lady when he sees one.'

Polly's blush deepened, the compliment a painful delight. 'Thank you, but I got the drift.' Self-conscious beneath his narrow-eyed scrutiny, she glanced out of the window again. Like a giant golden disc, the sun was sliding into the sea, turning it to blood. The sky above it burned orange and flame. But while the upper edges of the thickening cloud were bright as polished brass, underneath they were a sullen purple.

Though the violent fiery colours seemed somehow to suit this ancient volcanic island, to Polly there was something ominous about them.

'That's quite a sight,' she murmured.

'It is indeed,' Nathan agreed softly. But when she

glanced at him she saw he was supporting his chin on one hand and gazing directly at her.

Her heart gave an erratic lurch. 'I meant the sunset.' She gestured.

Reluctantly he turned his head. Watching him, Polly saw his jaw tighten, but all he said was, 'It looks as if we might be in for another blow.'

Polly could have hit him. It wasn't so much that he had confirmed her fears, it was his tone she found infuriating. He could afford to be casual about the odd Force Nine. He had years of sailing experience behind him. She glanced up. He was watching her.

'Don't worry,' he reassured her. '*Seawitch* can handle anything.'

Polly made a face. 'It's not *Seawitch* I'm worried about.'

His smile made her toes curl. 'I have complete faith in you.'

He'd said that as though he really meant it. Thrilled, but trying not to let it show, she darted him a look from under her lashes. 'And my one functioning grey cell?'

He winked. 'Added to my millions it bonds us into a formidable team.'

Polly was suddenly so happy she wanted to shout and sing. She wasn't a nuisance or a liability any more. She and Nathan were a *team*.

Then she gasped, her hand flying to her mouth. 'Lord, I nearly forgot. I started to tell you earlier, but you dashed off.'

'So tell me now,' he suggested, smiling briefly at the owner, who had returned with a steaming dish of tiny new potatoes sprinkled with chopped mint, and a shallow wooden bowl containing a salad of crisp endive, sliced cucumber, radicchio, olives, and chopped tomatoes.

Beaming, Paolo murmured in his thick Sicilian dialect words which Polly took to mean 'enjoy your meal', then waddled back to the kitchen.

Suddenly she wasn't sure. 'It probably doesn't mean anything. I expect it's just coincidence. After all, you said yourself——'

Nathan put down his knife and fork and leaned forward. 'Perhaps I'd be able to contribute something if I knew what you were talking about.'

'Not what, *who*.' Polly glanced over her shoulder. No one else had come in, yet she automatically lowered her voice. Which just goes to show how an overload of stress can make you totally irrational, she thought fleetingly.

'I saw him when I was leaving the market. He was with two other men. They looked like bankers or accountants.'

'For the love of God, Polly,' Nathan controlled himself with an effort, '*who* did you see?'

'That awful little man from Gibraltar. The one who stopped at our table and was so falsely sympathetic.' She shuddered.

Nathan's smile vanished. 'Louis?'

Polly nodded.

'You're certain it was him?'

'Positive,' she said at once.

'*Damn!*' Nathan exploded with quiet violence. 'Did he see you?'

She shook her head. 'No. I'm sure he didn't. I was behind a group of people.' She frowned. 'How do you suppose he got here? There isn't another yacht on the pontoon. I don't remember seeing one in the harbour either.'

'There's an airfield a few miles north, between here and Trapani.'

She shook her head in bewilderment. 'But your original plan was to go to Ibiza. How could he possibly know you would be coming here?'

Nathan looked up at her, his strong features set, his gaze diamond-hard. 'He didn't. Louis isn't here because of me. He's come to meet with his backers.'

Polly was even more puzzled. 'In *Sicily*?'

Nathan's fleeting smile was bleak. 'I told you there have always been a lot of unanswered questions about Louis. Like how he started his business empire, where the money came from. Many of us had our suspicions, but because he covered his tracks so well no one has ever been able to prove anything. You could say his being here is simply coincidence, but I think not.'

Polly shrugged helplessly. 'I don't understand.'

'Surely you've heard of the Cosa Nostra? Otherwise known as the Brotherhood?'

She shook her head.

He gave a small impatient sigh. 'The Mafia, Polly.'

She stared at him, wide-eyed. He was teasing her. No, he wasn't—one glance at his chilling expression convinced her of that. She could hardly believe what she'd heard. Yet why not? In the past week she had been arrested, charged with smuggling heroin, released on bail, learned how to sail a forty-foot yacht, and was now listening to the man she had fallen deeply and irrevocably in love with talk about his colleague's connection with the most vicious and widespread criminal organisation in the world. She gulped hard, struggling to suppress the impulse to laugh, knowing that if she gave in to it she would not be able to stop.

'I'm not sure whether Louis knows *Seawitch* is my boat,' Nathan said, 'but we can't take that chance. If,

by some appalling stroke of bad luck, he and I hap-
pened to bump into each other while we're here——'
He broke off. 'Well, it's better we don't, that's all.
We'll leave tonight.'

'But what about the radio?' Polly had total faith in
Nathan's seamanship, but they still had a lot of ocean
to cross, and the radio was a source of vital information
regarding sea and weather conditions.

His mouth curled in a silent snarl of frustration.

'We *could* manage without it, but—— No, I've got
a better idea. We'll move *Seawitch* along the coast.
She'll be out of sight, and so will we until I can pick
up the replacement set.' He paused, glancing out at
the sky.

The blaze of sunset had faded, leaving the sky
coloured like a huge bruise as crimson and purple
paled to light green and oyster. A thick dark blanket
of cloud with torn ragged edges was moving slowly
across the sky.

'If the weather doesn't break first,' he murmured.

The wind had died away and the throb of *Seawitch*'s
diesel engine seemed loud to Polly as Nathan guided
the boat out of the harbour.

She had been prepared to leave the restaurant at
once, but Nathan had insisted they finish their meal.

'If we rush away now, our host is going to be
curious,' he'd pointed out. 'And someone asking questions might just jog his memory.'

So they had followed their main course with *torta di
albicocche*, a sweet pastry case filled with apricots in a
creamy egg custard.

'That was absolutely delicious,' Polly had sighed,
spooning up the last crumb, amazed that the extra
pressure had not completely destroyed her appetite.
Maybe, she told herself, there was a limit to the

number of shocks a person could take. Perhaps a sort of protective emotional numbness set in. But not when she thought about Nathan.

'What was it flavoured with?' she'd asked hurriedly. 'I've never tasted anything like that before.'

The corners of Nathan's mouth had twitched. 'Marsala.'

'*Wine*?' She'd gazed at her plate, then at him.

'See what you've been missing?' He'd wagged a finger at her as she opened her mouth. 'You said it was delicious,' he had reminded her.

She had closed her mouth again. 'Mmm.' There wasn't anything else she could say.

As soon as they had emptied their tiny cups of black coffee, Nathan had settled the bill and they had walked quickly back down the hill to the waterfront.

'We should be all right here,' he said, bringing *Seawitch* into the shelter of a small, high-sided cove. Dusk was thickening into darkness, unbroken by any lights along this part of the shore.

Half an hour later *Seawitch* was anchored, the engine was silent, and Nathan had switched off the bow, stern, and masthead lights. 'No point in wasting the batteries,' he said as he pulled the hatch cover across, then pulled the doors closed.

Or letting anyone know we're here, Polly thought. A tremor shook her hand and the kettle she was filling clattered against the tap. She tried to hold it steady.

It wasn't the possibility of Louis learning of their presence in the town that was making her so nervous. It was the thought of the next fifteen hours. There was no meal to prepare, no chores to catch up on, no watches to keep. She had to do *something*.

Putting the kettle down on the worktop, she hurried past the ladder before Nathan reached the bottom.

'Where are you going?' he demanded.

'T-to g-get my n-navigation notes,' she stammered the words over her shoulder. 'I l-left them on the locker.' She hurried down the passage.

As she picked up the notebook she heard a sound close behind her and jerked round. Nathan stood in the doorway, filling the narrow space. 'Why do you want those?' he asked.

Polly looked at her scribbled notes, then shrugged. 'It seems like a good time to——' At the cynical lift of his eyebrows her voice trailed off.

Silently he took the notebook from her nerveless fingers and dropped it on the floor.

She could feel the edge of the bed pressing against the backs of her legs. Say something, she told herself. But no words would come.

Nathan's gaze flickered over her, his own thoughts hidden behind eyes reflecting the soft glow of the bedhead lamp. His hands came up to rest on her shoulders. Their warm weight made her stomach quake. She stared at his throat, hypnotised by the pulse beating beneath the bronzed skin. As his hands slid down her upper arms and he drew her slowly but inexorably towards him, her throat grew dry.

No. That was all she had to say. And he would stop—he had before.

His lips brushed her forehead, then her temple. 'No more running, Polly,' he whispered.

Her eyes closed and she turned her head to one side. *Not her mouth.* If he touched her mouth then she would be lost. But this—this she could handle. She couldn't fight, but she wouldn't respond.

His lips traced the curve of her cheekbone to her ear, then followed the line of her jaw. And though the kisses were feather-light, his grip on her arms tightened as his breathing grew deeper and more ragged.

She swallowed convulsively. Her skin tingled and her heart thumped wildly as he moved closer. Her hands flew to his shoulders, but whether to fend him off or make him stay she could not have said. Then, as her quick intake of breath parted her lips, in one smooth, sweeping movement he wrapped his arms around her, holding her so close, so tight, that she could barely breathe.

From chest to thigh she burned. Clothes were no barrier to awareness. Nathan's powerful body was taut and hard with his need for her. He was both conqueror and supplicant.

Beyond her control, her body arched against his and she gasped. The honey-sweet warmth that had smouldered deep inside her exploded, filling her with a shimmering liquid heat.

His head came down and his mouth took hers, not gentle now but fierce and demanding. His tongue touched, stroked, explored, hot, supple and silky.

His hand spread across the small of her back, moulding her to him. And she trembled, yielding, softening, flowering against him as a slowly swirling vortex of yearning began to build to an urgency.

She whimpered, the wordless sound lost in their hungry mouths and mingled breath. She wanted him as he wanted her. She wanted to belong, to be part of, to be loved by this man. And if tonight was all there was, all there ever would be, then she would take it and be glad.

She felt herself lifted. Then the mattress was under her back, softened by the double thickness of the sleeping-bags.

As she returned kiss for kiss, sure of nothing but her

need for him, she felt his hand free her hair where it clung to her hot damp skin, then glide lightly down.

She stopped breathing. But Nathan continued to stroke, his light touch soothing yet irresistible. Her arms crept around his neck, her lips softened and parted beneath his and she slid into a world of sensation so subtle and exquisite that it was almost too much to bear.

She clung to him, vaguely aware of movement and soft rustling. She felt a fleeting distant surprise as the cool night air whispered over her skin. But then he covered her, his naked body burning hot, heavy but not crushing, strong and powerful. And gentle, always gentle.

She sensed him holding back, waiting, but for what she didn't know. She arched, opened, welcomed. The vortex had tightened into a spiral that was winding tighter and tighter. Her arms tensed around his neck, across his back, as tiny frenzied shudderings shook her.

He held her very close, and with hands and lips calmed and soothed. And suddenly, in the midst of the turmoil, everything steadied and locked into a slow relentless rhythm. Deep and powerful, driving and urgent, the wave lifted her, carried her forward, drew back to gather force, then surged forward again, higher. And again. Then it was different. This time the wave didn't recede, this time it built, went on building, higher and higher.

Polly cried out, clutching Nathan's shoulders. He gave a hoarse groan. Then the wave curled, broke, and fell. An endless falling through time and space, and ecstasy so intense that she thought she would die. It ebbed gently like the tide, leaving her stranded, plundered, boneless.

She felt the bed move. Suddenly she was cold and realised distantly that Nathan had gone from her. She tried to protest, to call him back, but the effort was too great and, as something light and warm was laid over her, she drifted into sleep.

CHAPTER TEN

POLLY lay quite still, eyes wide open, listening intently. She had grown used to the tiny sounds that were so much a part of *Seawitch*, just as she had grown used to the boat's continually changing motion. So what had woken her?

She stretched and winced. Memories overwhelmed her and her whole body flushed and tingled. All of a sudden the cabin seemed stiflingly hot.

She grasped the light covering and was about to throw it off when she realised from the fabric's texture that her own cotton skirt had been laid over her. Beneath it she was naked.

She felt different, and explored this new pleasure-drugged and peaceful self. Though she was stiff and slightly sore, the tension that had made her talk too much, drop things, and jump at the smallest unexpected noise had completely disappeared. She felt heavy and languid.

She stretched again, arching her body and extending her limbs like a contented cat. She reached out to switch on the bedhead light and realised that the blackness of night had been replaced by grey gloom. How long had she slept?

After she had pulled on her baggy T-shirt, shyness made her step into her skirt before she opened the cabin door. She was thirsty and wanted a drink. But more than that, more than anything else in the world, she wanted to be with Nathan.

Fully expecting to see him either in the saloon, or in

the galley, she was surprised to find both empty. She knew he wasn't in the head, because she had gone in herself to wash her face and hands and rake a comb through her wildly disordered hair.

The girl in the mirror was a total contrast to the haunted image which had stared back at her a few hours earlier. Where that one had been tense and drawn, this one was soft and rosy, warm and sensuous.

Polly looked up the companionway ladder. Both the hatch and the doors were closed. Yet where else could he be but on deck? Perhaps he'd wanted some fresh air. Even with the hatches open, with no breeze blowing the cabins quickly became humid and the air heavy.

She climbed up the ladder, the rungs cold under her bare feet, pushed open the unbolted doors and stepped out into the cockpit. It was empty.

Her smile faded and a shaft of panic shot through her. *Seawitch*'s stern swung round, her bow held fast by the anchor chain as a sudden gust of wind caught her. Polly shivered. The weather was changing already. Was that what had woken her?

She grabbed the handhold on the coach roof to steady herself and looked round wildly. Where was he? Then she heard splashing.

Leaning over the side and straining her eyes in the pre-dawn light, she scanned the sea. 'Nathan?' she cried, her voice snatched by the rising wind.

'Be quiet!' His hissed order came from just beyond the stern. 'What are you trying to do? Wake the entire island?'

Guilt suffused her. The whole purpose of moving along here was to be as inconspicuous as possible. 'Sorry,' she whispered back. Then she caught her breath as he appeared over the transom, his lean, dripping figure a more solid shape in the gloom. Her body relived the wondrous things he had done, and she felt weak inside.

'What are you doing up here anyway?' he demanded, leaning over to pick up the towel he had left on the seat. 'You should be asleep.'

'I was,' she said, hugging her arms around her. Was it just the rising wind that was chilling her, making her tremble? 'But,' she shrugged shyly, 'I wondered where you'd gone.'

He had finished rubbing his face and head, and was drying his arms and chest. 'I needed——' He broke off and, lowering his arms, fastened the towel around his hips.

It was only then that Polly realised he was naked. She felt her face grow warm, and immediately ridiculed her shyness. Only a short time ago she had been as physically intimate with him as it was possible for a man and woman to be. That magnificent body had become part of hers. He had taken her into another dimension.

It had been too incredible for words to describe. She had been demolished, yet made whole, complete. Yet she sensed that was only a beginning. To really know him would take a lifetime.

But would she have that long? Something wasn't right. He had distanced himself from her. *Why*? Fear wound itself like clammy tentacles around her heart and slithered along her veins. Was he regretting what had happened between them?

Seawitch tugged at her line again, pitching on the rising swell. The gust was stronger this time.

'Go below,' Nathan ordered. His curt tone made her stomach lurch.

She moistened lips that still felt tender and slightly

bruised from his kisses. 'Not until you tell me what's wrong.'

'The weather's breaking,' he said impatiently. 'I thought we'd be OK here until later in the morning, but the wind has shifted.'

'I wasn't talking about the weather,' Polly began.

'Listen to me,' he interrupted harshly. 'If I don't get *Seawitch* moved we could well end up as wreckage on those rocks.' Grasping her shoulders, he moved her aside to open the doors. His hands were cold, his touch impersonal. 'The weather is *now*. Everything else must wait. Go and put something warm on.'

She didn't want to leave him. 'What about you? Can I——?'

'My clothes are here.' He gestured towards one corner of the moulded seat. 'I'll be down in a moment. Go on.' He moved her firmly towards the hatchway.

Though she recognised the logic and understood the urgency, her unease blossomed first into anxiety, then dread. Polly turned and went down the ladder.

He was like a stranger. Where was the man she had lain with and loved such a short while ago? He had been so gentle, controlling his own need while he readied her with exquisite subtlety and patience. And she had bloomed and flowered beneath a touch that she sensed deep in her innermost self was not simply skill and experience, but a kind of homage to womanhood. He had recognised and understood the value of the gift she offered, and had taken it with reverence and respect. He had made *love* to her. But now?

Now he was behaving as though he wished she were somewhere—anywhere—else. There was far more behind this than just a deterioration in the weather. What had she done? What hadn't she done? Something was dreadfully wrong. Why wouldn't he *tell* her?

Re-entering the cabin, she noticed how it smelled of them, of the mingled scents of their bodies, of the soaps they used, and the sweet, musky afterglow of love.

Swallowing her fear, Polly wiped her wet eyes with the back of her hand, then quickly pulled on jeans, a shirt, and her thick Aran cardigan. No longer warm and relaxed, she felt tense and cold.

'How much longer are you going to be?' Nathan yelled down the passage.

'I'm coming right now,' she shouted back, pushing her blue-socked feet into her trainers.

Nathan was hauling the oilskins out of the locker as she turned the corner.

'OK, I'm ready.' Her brisk normality took every ounce of will-power she had. 'What do you want me to do?'

Slamming the locker door shut, he started towards the saloon. Polly followed, devouring the tall, broad-shouldered figure with her eyes.

'I think,' he half turned his head to speak over his shoulder, his voice a rasp, devoid of expression, 'I think it would be better if I put you ashore.' He didn't meet her eyes.

Polly's blood turned to ice. Just a few hours ago this had been exactly what she wanted. But everything had changed since then.

Her lower lip stung and burned where her teeth pierced it. She shook her head quickly. 'You can't mean it. We're a team, you said so yourself. With the weather changing—we've got to move *Seawitch*—you need me to—— And what about food? Neither of us has eaten since last night.' Realising she was babbling, she started towards the galley. 'I'll go and——'

'You'll stop arguing and do as you're damned well

told!' he roared, his face bleak, his eyes as hard and cold as granite.

'Nathan, don't——' Her whole body seemed to be shrinking into itself, trying to escape the pain that threatened to engulf it. 'I c—can't leave——' *You*. The word trembled on the tip of her tongue, but she choked it back just in time. 'I can't leave *Seawitch*. You said so. The conditions of bail——'

'Forget the bloody bail,' he rasped, white-lipped. 'You don't owe me a penny. Clive Kemp confessed. He confirmed that you knew nothing about any of it. The charges against you have been dropped. You don't have to go back to Gibraltar. You don't have to stay with me. You're free.'

A loud buzzing filled Polly's head and everything around her started to recede. She clutched at the companionway ladder, fighting nausea as she clung desperately to consciousness. 'When——? How long have you——?'

'Does it matter?' He looked away, his jaw clenched.

Perspiration dewed her face. Her clothes stuck clammily to her shivering body. She raised her head. 'You bastard,' she whispered. Nathan flinched. 'You said—you made me believe—— It was all a lie, wasn't it? Everything. Last night. . .' Her voice cracked.

Nathan was visibly shaken. 'Polly, listen, about last night——'

She shrank away from him, one hand pressed to her chest. The pain was crucifying. She was breaking apart inside. 'It didn't mean anything, did it? Just a little bit of light relief to liven up a dull voyage.'

'*No*,' he thundered, growing pale. 'You can't believe that.'

'Why not?' She threw the words at him, then sucked in a shuddering breath, dashing a hand across her wet cheeks. 'I thought you were interested in me as a person, interested in what I felt and believed. You certainly asked enough questions. You said I was intelligent and beautiful, and I actually started to believe you. See what a fool I am? But as I've never played this game before I didn't know the rules.'

'What rules? What are you talking about?' he demanded.

'That I wasn't supposed to take it seriously. That the compliments were just part of the softening-up process.' Scalding tears poured down her face. 'God knows I should have had more sense. Your work is the centre of your life.' She hurled the words at him, her body taut with anguish. 'No matter how hard I tried I could never reach your standards. And you made it perfectly clear that nothing less would do. So I was just a bit of sport. Something to pass the time and ease the boredom. All you wanted was the thrill of the chase.' The enormity of his betrayal wrenched a choking sob from her. 'Did I give you a good run for your money? Did I?'

His eyes glittered like splinters of steel. 'Stop that,' he hissed. 'Stop it at once.'

Overwhelmed by her pain, Polly barely heard him. 'But once caught, the prey's of no further interest.'

Nathan's face was ashen. 'That's not true.'

'No, of course it isn't,' she mocked him bitterly. 'That's why you want to get rid of me.'

'Will you listen to me? You've got it wrong.' He started towards her.

Grasping the ladder, she looked over her shoulder at him, naked grief stark on her face. 'No, I haven't. Come on, why waste time? Let's get *Seawitch* moving.'

'Polly, wait. Come back!' Raw urgency sharpened Nathan's voice.

Ignoring him, Polly scrambled up the ladder and out into driving rain. As she wrestled with the winches, hauling in the anchor and unfurling the headsail, her upper arms were seized in a vice-like grip.

Nathan spun her round. 'What in the name of God do you think you're doing?' His eyes blazed as anger chiselled his features into an unrecognisable mask. The rain plastered his thick hair to his magnificent head and streamed down his face, which looked ashen in the grey light.

Teeth chattering, her whole body trembling uncontrollably, Polly tried to wrench free. 'If we don't move *Seawitch* she could end up as wreckage on the rocks—that's what you said. Besides, you want to put me ashore, so unless you expect me to swim——' She broke off, gasping as the boat, no longer held fast by its anchor, swung wildly. She was pulled from Nathan's grasp and staggered backwards. She saw his expression change, the fury replaced by fear.

'Sweetheart, look out!' He lunged forward and caught her shoulder. As *Seawitch* rolled heavily Polly's foot slipped on the wet deck and she stumbled backwards, pulling Nathan with her. The heavy boom swung across, catching him high on the left side of his forehead. He gave a sharp cry. His knees buckled and he slumped unconscious to the floor of the cockpit, his head lolling against the moulded seat.

'Nathan!' Polly cried, grabbing the wheel as *Seawitch* bucked and heaved beneath them. *Sweetheart*. He had called her *sweetheart*. And in saving her *he* had been hurt.

His eyes were closed and pallor gave his weathered tan a peculiar blotchy look. A thin trickle of blood from the rapidly swelling bruise blurred to pale pink, diluted by the pounding rain.

Ice-cold, shocked, her stomach a tight knot of abject terror, Polly gazed wildly around her. Her mouth opened to scream for help, but the sound emerged as a strangled groan as she realised the mind-numbing truth.

There *was* no help. With Nathan unconscious, the responsibility was hers. If she lost control of the boat they would both be drowned. She had to get them away from the rocks that edged the shore like jagged teeth.

She couldn't do it. She didn't know enough. Yes, she did. Hadn't Nathan trusted her to take her turn at the helm while he slept? Both their lives were in her hands. Which was greater? Her fear? Or her love for him?

Adrenalin surged through her veins, clearing her mind and filling her with determination. They had to survive. She had to know the truth. What had he been trying to tell her? If he had simply been using her why, in that split-second of warning, had he called her sweetheart?

Discovering strength and skills she hadn't known she possessed, Polly sailed *Seawitch* away from the wave-lashed rocky coast and out into the safety of deeper water.

A sudden drop in the wind told her the worst was over. The rain stopped like a tap being turned off. Then the heavy cloud began to break up and the pearly rays of the morning sun beamed down on a spume-streaked sea that glistened in shades of emerald and jade.

Polly lifted her cold wet face to the welcome warmth, weak with relief and gratitude. Gathering her remaining strength, she engaged the auto-helm and, dragging the first-aid kit out of the locker under the seat, knelt beside Nathan.

As she gently pushed his dripping hair back, her fingers lingered on his broad forehead. Beneath the wetness of the rain his skin was warm. He stirred, groaning softly. She felt her heart swell, so full of love for him that it ached, and, blinking back the tears that blurred and fragmented his image, she drew in a deep, steadying breath and examined the wound.

It had stopped bleeding and the rain had washed it clean. Already bruising had coloured the egg-sized lump red and purple. Tearing some cotton wool off a roll, Polly carefully wiped the area dry. Nathan's face tightened in a wince and he muttered something unintelligible as she smoothed on some antiseptic cream. Quickly wiping her fingers on the cotton wool, she tore a large plaster from its paper envelope and pressed the dressing into place over the lacerated bump.

During his lessons on seamanship, Nathan had warned her about the dangers of leaving cuts untreated. Constant exposure to seawater, far from having a healing effect, actually caused boils and other skin infections.

How much she had learned from him. In just a few days he had pushed back the horizons of her world far out of sight. It had been a baptism by fire, but she had come through. No longer a girl with a headful of hazy dreams, she was a woman now. Maybe grief was the price of wisdom and maturity.

Gathering up the debris, she stuffed it into her pocket to dispose of in the galley bin below. As she returned the first-aid box to the locker, she heard a movement behind her and glanced round.

Nathan was frowning as he gingerly touched the plaster.

Polly knelt beside him, her grin uncertain. 'Welcome back.' Now the crisis was over she felt utterly drained.

Soaked to the skin and chilled to the marrow of her bones, she shivered uncontrollably.

He gazed at her. 'You weren't hurt?'

She shook her dripping head. 'It hit you instead.'

His forehead furrowed with fierce concentration. She could almost see his brain working. Suddenly his eyes widened and he lunged forward. 'The rocks——'

'It's all right.' Polly grabbed his shoulders, holding him back. 'There's no danger. We're well away from the coast.' She helped him up on to the seat, then sagged down beside him, forearms resting on her knees, head bent, dizzy from the exertion. She felt rather than saw him gazing round, trying to work out what had happened.

'How long was I out?' he asked.

Trying to smooth the tension from her face with both hands, she shrugged. 'I'm not sure.'

'You didn't notice?' His sharp irony was tempered by amazement.

'I was rather busy,' she flared. 'If anything had happened to your precious boat, or we'd both drowned, you'd never have let me forget——' Her voice trailed off as she recognised the absurdity of what she was saying.

'Too right,' he snapped. 'I'd have haunted you from here to eternity.'

'You'll do that anyway,' she retorted, then looked away quickly, knowing she'd betrayed herself. She stood up too fast, grabbing the coaming as dizziness made her sway. 'I—I'll—we both need a hot drink.'

He rose to his feet, blocking the companionway with

his body. Already he looked his old strong, capable self. His colour had returned to normal. He shook his head slowly. 'Polly Levington, you are one hell of a woman.'

Jerking her head up, Polly stared at him, not quite certain how to react, for his tone hadn't been one of admiration, but more a reluctant acknowledgement.

'Thanks,' she said drily. 'But what's a spell of bad weather between fr——?' She broke off again, turning her head aside. She moistened her lips, feeling the raised and tender flesh where her teeth had bitten through.

Friends. That was what she had been going to say. Despite all the sparks they had struck off one another she had felt they were forging a deep friendship based on mutual respect and acknowledgement of each other's special qualities. But that had been before——

'Excuse me,' she whispered, and tried to push past him.

He didn't budge. Instead he caught her chin and raised it, forcing her to meet his eyes. 'I owe you my life,' he said softly.

She shook her head. 'No, you don't owe me a thing.' She wanted him to understand. 'When death was a distinct possibility, I realised just how precious life really is. It might not hold all I'd hoped for, but. . .' She made a brief gesture of acceptance. 'And in certain ways I've been very lucky. At least I've known what——' She broke off, unable to continue. 'There's just one thing.' She swallowed the lump in her throat. 'Please, I have to know. When did you learn about Clive's confession?'

Nathan glanced at his watch. 'About fifteen hours ago.'

Polly's eyes widened. 'But—I thought——'

'Yes,' he said drily, 'I know. And I didn't get the chance to explain. The message came through just before you arrived back with the shopping. I intended to tell you last evening, but what with one thing and another——' He released her chin and slid his fingers up the side of her face to cup it.

Polly's mouth felt parched. Her heartbeat was wild and erratic. Her skin beneath his fingers burned. She wanted to close her eyes and rub her face against his hand. 'Why, Nathan?' The words burst from her. 'Why did you freeze me out?' Her eyes beseeched him for the truth.

His face hardened and for one dreadful moment she thought he was going to turn away. Then she realised. The contempt that narrowed his eyes and thinned his mouth was not directed at her, but at himself.

'I was ashamed,' he said bluntly. 'I took advantage of your lack of experience.'

Polly brows drew together. 'No, you didn't. I could have said no.'

His eyes bored into hers. 'Could you?' he demanded drily. 'Once I'd begun to make love to you, could you really have asked me to stop?'

'Well, perhaps not,' she admitted.

'Exactly.'

'But I didn't want you to stop,' she added quickly. '*I* didn't want to stop. It felt too wonderful, too *right*.'

A muscle jumped in Nathan's jaw. 'From the moment I met you I liked your spirit, and I was strongly attracted to you. But I wasn't—I hadn't thought beyond that.'

She swallowed. 'That's OK. I understand.' She tried to smile. 'Look, it takes two. And I was—what do they call it?—the other consenting adult in the affair.' The smile faltered, the strain too great.

'Polly, you can't call one—episode—an affair.' His voice flattened, becoming harsher. 'Besides, what happened with us would never, could never, be that. Not now.'

Polly met his troubled gaze. She had to hear it from his own lips, even if it meant that part of her died. At least she would finally know the truth. 'Why not now, Nathan? Have you decided you're not cut out for a permanent relationship? That you prefer being alone? Is that why you wanted to put me ashore?'

His brief smile held no humour. 'On the contrary.'

She watched him, hardly daring to breathe, let alone hope.

He paused, and she sensed him gathering his thoughts. 'When I bullied you into accepting my terms to get you out of gaol, my only concern was reaching Athens in time for my meeting.'

His gaze shifted, and he stared into the distance, his expression cruelly self-mocking. But his fingers moved lightly, continuously, stroking the side of her face. And Polly had the strange feeling that he was drawing comfort from touching her.

'I needed a crew who could cook. Though you were decidedly naïve, you had guts and were obviously intelligent. I have to admit I was also physically attracted to you. The idea of a brief fling certainly crossed my mind. But Polly, I'm not the Casanova the gossip columns would have you believe. It had been a long time since I——' He broke off. 'Well, that's hardly relevant now.'

He looked down at her, his expression softening as he studied her uptilted face. 'What I hadn't considered,' he said softly, 'what had never occurred to me, was that I might fall in love with you.'

Polly suddenly felt extraordinarily light, as if she

was floating. She hadn't realised that grief could be a physical weight. Not until it fell away, sloughed off like a dead skin.

Her heart in her eyes, she made a wry face. 'You certainly managed to hide it well.'

The corners of his mouth curved upward. 'That's because, being a stranger to the emotion, I didn't recognise it.'

'Not even when we——?' Polly bit her lip. She hadn't meant to ask, the words had just slipped out.

He shook his head gently. 'Not until afterwards. And it hit me like a thunderbolt. That's why I left you. It was one hell of a thing to come to terms with.'

'Yet you wanted to put me ashore.' The desperate hurt she had felt coloured her voice.

His face darkened. 'Oh, Polly,' he whispered, and, sliding his fingers through her wet hair to support her head, he kissed her parted lips with infinite tenderness. But it quickly bloomed into passion.

As her arms went around his neck he held her close. He raised his head and looked down into her eyes. 'I was afraid for you—of you. It was a knee-jerk reaction. You'd got to me. I hadn't expected it. I wasn't prepared for it. I can't deny I've met a lot of women. Or rather, they've set out to meet me. I even imagined myself in love once.'

Polly felt a sharp pang of jealousy. Then it dawned on her that Nathan's tone held bitterness rather than admiration.

'She had model-girl looks, a soft sweet way of talking, and seemed really interested in my work. I thought that at last I'd found someone I could share my life with. I trusted her, confided in her.' His features grew bleak. 'Then I found out that I came a poor second to the real love of her life—money. While declaring undying love for me she'd been busy making herself a small fortune giving kiss-and-tell interviews to some tabloid rag.' His smile was bitter. 'I decided to give *love* a miss after that.'

Polly smoothed the tumbled curls off his forehead, careful to avoid the plaster-covered wound. 'Oh, Nathan,' she whispered, 'I'm so sorry.'

He shook his head. 'And I had the gall to judge you by those standards. Can you forgive me?'

Pressing her lips to his cheek, she smiled. 'Do you really need to ask?'

'I've never known a woman like you.' Behind the awe in his gaze a deeper, more powerful emotion smouldered, sending thrills like tiny flames along her nerve-ends. 'You have as much courage as any man I know. You'll work until you're literally dropping with tiredness. You'll fight for what you believe in. Yet you can be so warm and gentle.' His voice sank to a rough murmur. 'So totally, beautifully feminine.' He rubbed the side of his face against her temple. The rasp of his beard stubble was a sweet pain.

'When we—I realised right away that I was the first man to. . . I should have stopped. But, God help me, I couldn't. You were—are—everything I ever dreamed a woman could be.'

'Oh, Nathan!' Polly gulped, her joy overflowing in tears of happiness.

'Just one thing,' he murmured several minutes later. 'After I got knocked out how the hell did you stop us from being driven on to the rocks?'

Knowing that Nathan's arms were the safest place in the world and the only security she would ever need, Polly smiled up at him and shrugged. 'I simply remembered what you'd told me and did that.'

His admiration was tinged with puzzlement. 'Weren't you frightened?'

She thought for a moment. 'I suppose so. But I was more worried about you. I didn't know how badly you were injured, but I didn't dare let go of the wheel.'

'After the way I'd behaved——'

She reached up and kissed him. 'I was hurt,' she admitted. 'But I loved—love—you. That wasn't conditional on you loving me.'

His arms tightened around her. 'You said my work is the centre of my life. It was, until I met you. I never thought I would ever find a woman who could mean as much. And when I did I behaved like a damned fool. I could have lost you.'

'It's all right, Nathan,' Polly reassured him. 'Everything's OK.'

Taking a deep breath, he made a visible effort to push the nightmare aside, and grinned down at her. 'Sure it is. We're soaking wet, dog-tired, and off course. As I'm not prepared to risk meeting Louis and his Mafia friends I can't go back to pick up the replacement VHF set—which means we might well be without radio contact all the way to Greece.'

'What will happen about Louis?' Polly asked. 'Will he be allowed to go on competing?'

'Not if I can help it.' Nathan's expression was grimly determined. 'I don't think it will take the investigators long to come up with enough to disqualify Louis from international yacht racing. Not now that we can suggest where they might start looking.'

Polly patted the sodden sweater stretched across his broad chest. 'Well, that's one less competitor you have to worry about. I'll go and put the kettle on.'

Nathan threw his head back and gave a great shout

of laughter. 'Woman, you're superb. When will you marry me?'

She looked thoughtfully up at him. 'Are you sure that's what you want, Nathan?'

He hugged her fiercely. 'Yes. Now I've found you I'm not going to risk losing you. Why? You haven't got any doubts, have you?'

The sudden tension in him wrenched her heart. 'No, my darling.' She smiled up at him. Knowing she was loved by this powerful, dictatorial, gentle, *wonderful* man wiped away all the wounds and hurts of the past. 'None at all.' She stroked his cheek.

He grinned. 'You'll like being married. You're going to be incredibly good at it—I can tell. In fact, I can hardly wait.'

'Then let's not wait,' Polly suggested.

Nathan looked puzzled. 'You mean—don't you want a big family wedding with all the trimmings?'

She shook her head. 'This is for us, Nathan, you and me. We're under no obligation to put on a show for other people's benefit.'

'In Greece, then? As soon as the meeting's over?'

The glow in his eyes made her heart swell, but she couldn't resist a gentle tease. 'With so many important things to do, will you have time?'

'I'll make time,' he threatened softly with a half-smile that sent shivers of delight along her spine. 'About a honeymoon——'

'I get one of those as well?'

'Of course. Any preferences?'

Polly grinned up at him. 'Well, as I'm just beginning to get the hang of this sailing business. . .'

His arms tightened around her. 'What would you say to a long leisurely cruise?' Her momentary uncertainty must have showed, for he added with a throaty chuckle, 'But no night watches.'

Polly drew her index finger across his lips and gasped as his teeth fastened gently on it. 'Mmm, I like the sound of that.'

'By the way——' Nathan said thoughtfully.

'Yes?' she murmured, fascinated by the blend of gentleness and passion in this powerfully masculine man.

He grazed her temple with warm lips, then raised his head so he could study her. 'I have to do a lot of travelling in the coming year. I want you with me. I couldn't possibly allow my wife to work for men who can't keep their minds on the job and their hands to themselves.' Though his expression was serious she recognised that gleam in his eye.

'Unless they happen to be you?' she finished drily.

'I've always admired your quick grasp of essentials.'

'We-ell——' she pretended to consider.

Nathan held her close. 'When I said before that I'd trust you with my life, it was a statement based on instinct. Now, I *know*. I want you with me, Polly. I want your professionalism and integrity at my side during working hours.' His voice deepened, and grew husky. 'And I want your very, very personal attention all night. Equal partners, a lifetime contract. What do you say?'

Polly laid her palms against the strong hard face she loved so much, knowing *exactly* what she wanted to do with the rest of her life. 'Nathan Bryce,' her smile reflected the radiance that filled her whole being, 'you've got yourself a deal.'

**Fifty red-blooded, white-hot, true-blue hunks
from every State in the Union!**

Look for MEN MADE IN AMERICA! Written by some
of our most poplar authors, these stories feature fifty of
the strongest, sexiest men, each from a different state in
the union!

Two titles available every other month at your favorite
retail outlet.

In November, look for:

**STRAIGHT FROM THE HEART by Barbara Delinsky
(Connecticut)
AUTHOR'S CHOICE by Elizabeth August (Delaware)**

In January, look for:

**DREAM COME TRUE by Ann Major (Florida)
WAY OF THE WILLOW by Linda Shaw (Georgia)**

You won't be able to resist MEN MADE IN AMERICA!

Make Christmas a truly
Romantic experience—with

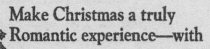 HARLEQUIN ROMANCE®

Wouldn't *you* love to kiss a tall, dark
Texan under the mistletoe? Gwen does,
in HOME FOR CHRISTMAS by
Ellen James. Share the experience!

Wouldn't *you* love to kiss a sexy
New Englander on a snowy Christmas
morning? Angela does, in Shannon
Waverly's CHRISTMAS ANGEL.
Share the experience!

Look for both of these Christmas
Romance titles, available in December
wherever Harlequin Books are sold.

(And don't forget that Romance novels
make great gifts! Easy to buy, easy to
wrap and just the right size for a
stocking stuffer. And they make a
wonderful treat when you need a break
from Christmas shopping, Christmas
wrapping and stuffing stockings!)

©OG 1990   HRXT

Harlequin is proud to present our best authors and their best books. Always the best for your reading pleasure!

Throughout 1993, Harlequin will bring you exciting books by some of the top names in contemporary romance!

In November, look for

BARBARA DELINSKY

First, Best and Only

Their passion burned even stronger....

CEO Marni Lange didn't have time for nonsense like photographs. The promotion department, however, insisted she was the perfect cover model for the launch of their new career-woman magazine. She couldn't argue with her own department. She should have.

The photographer was a man she'd prayed never to see again. Brian Webster had been her first— and best—lover. This time, could she play with fire without being burned?

Don't miss FIRST, BEST AND ONLY by Barbara Delinsky... wherever Harlequin books are sold.

BOB6

1993 Keepsake

CHRISTMAS

Stories

Capture the spirit and romance of Christmas with KEEPSAKE CHRISTMAS STORIES, a collection of three stories by favorite historical authors. The perfect Christmas gift!

Don't miss these heartwarming stories, available in November wherever Harlequin books are sold:

ONCE UPON A CHRISTMAS by Curtiss Ann Matlock
A FAIRYTALE SEASON by Marianne Willman
TIDINGS OF JOY by Victoria Pade

ADD A TOUCH OF ROMANCE TO YOUR HOLIDAY SEASON WITH KEEPSAKE CHRISTMAS STORIES!

HX93

When the only time you have for yourself is...

Christmas is such a busy time—with shopping, decorating, writing cards, trimming trees, wrapping gifts....

When you do have a few *stolen moments* to call your own, treat yourself to a brand-new *short* novel. Relax with one of our Stocking Stuffers—or with all six!

Each STOLEN MOMENTS title
is a complete and original contemporary romance that's the perfect length for the busy woman of the nineties! Especially at Christmas...

And they make perfect **stocking stuffers**, too! (For your mother, grandmother, daughters, friends, co-workers, neighbors, aunts, cousins—all the other women in your life!)

Look for the STOLEN MOMENTS display in December

STOCKING STUFFERS:

HIS MISTRESS Carrie Alexander
DANIEL'S DECEPTION Marie DeWitt
SNOW ANGEL Isolde Evans
THE FAMILY MAN Danielle Kelly
THE LONE WOLF Ellen Rogers
MONTANA CHRISTMAS Lynn Russell

HSM2

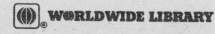 **WORLDWIDE LIBRARY**